S0-AQL-373

6/04

S

BURNING
PRECINCT PUERTO RICO

BURNING
PRECINCT PUERTO RICO

BOOK THREE

STEVEN TORRES

THOMAS DUNNE BOOKS

ST. MARTIN'S MINOTAUR ✿ NEW YORK

3 1969 01504 3689

THOMAS DUNNE BOOKS.
An imprint of St. Martin's Press.

BURNING PRECINCT PUERTO RICO: BOOK THREE. Copyright © 2004 by
Steven Torres. All rights reserved. Printed in the United States of America. No
part of this book may be used or reproduced in any manner whatsoever without written permission except in the case of brief quotations embodied in
critical articles or reviews. For information, address St. Martin's Press,
175 Fifth Avenue, New York, N.Y. 10010.

www.minotaurbooks.com

Library of Congress Cataloging-in-Publication Data

Torres, Steven.
    Burning precinct Puerto Rico : a Luis Gonzalo novel / Steven
Torres.— 1st ed.
      p. cm.
    "Book three."
    ISBN 0-312-32109-0
    EAN 978-0312-32109-3
    1. Gonzalo, Luis (Fictitious character)—Fiction. 2. Police—Puerto
Rico—Fiction. 3. Arson investigation—Fiction. 4. Puerto Rico—
Fiction.   I. Title.
PS3620.O59B87   2004
813'.6—dc22

                            2003069451

First Edition: May 2004

10 9 8 7 6 5 4 3 2 1

This book is dedicated
to

Annie, Tita, Juni,
Telly, Lizzy, Naomi,
Fije, Pina, and Monin.
Together in one room, the greatest storytelling machine on Earth.

To
Tat Sang So,
who prods me to tell the best story I can.

To
Marcia Markland,
who likes my stories and tells everyone.

And, of course,
to
Damaris,
my love.

BURNING
PRECINCT PUERTO RICO

HORNETS' NEST

PROLOGUE

When you destroy a hornets' nest, be sure to kill all the hornets."
This was the first lesson Pedro learned about dealing with hornets,
and he had learned it the hard way. The first time his father let him
handle a hornets' nest alone, Pedro had run out of the woods with a
total of six hornet stings on his face and arms; he was thirteen. The
marks on his cheek and forehead stayed with him the longest, sur-
viving into his early manhood. Now in his thirties, he approached
the task with caution on the land he had inherited from his father.
The afternoon before, he had found a thriving hive on the underside
of a coffee tree leaf. It was almost time for harvest, and the nest had
to go.

Pedro walked through the cool of the shady woods. He carried
all the tools he would need: a broomstick, a paper bag filled with
crumpled newspaper, a bit of twine, and a box of matches. He also

1

carried a machete, its blade filed down to an inch in width and the handle held together with black electrician's tape. This, for some vines he had seen growing on an orange tree.

The temperature at that hour made the hornets a bit more drowsy, less eager to attack, easier to kill. He noticed a termite mud tube forming on a young avocado tree. He would disrupt it on his way back. All avocado trees were susceptible, and termites usually killed the trees in the end, but scraping away their tunnels could help get a few more years of fruit and the exposed insects fed the lizards.

Pedro found the tree he wanted. The hive was just then coming to life. It was the size of a grapefruit and held about twenty or twenty-five hornets at the moment. Pedro figured a couple might be away from the hive, but they would return to find the hive melted, the leaf blackened and curled, their comrades dead.

Pedro stood about a half-dozen feet from the nest and tied the paper bag to the end of the broomstick. He ripped a hole into the bag to expose the newspaper inside, lit a match, and started a fire. He held the broomstick handle short until the flames were licking out of the bag, letting the smoke curl around his face. When the flames had reached their peak intensity, he took the broomstick by its end and engulfed the hive in an inferno from underneath, picking the hive from off his plant. He let the bag burn for another minute. A hornet, returning from whatever reconnaissance it had been doing, buzzed past his ear and neared the place where the nest had been. Pedro singed it in midair with what was left of the flames. Then he stamped on the bag once or twice though the fire was out already. With his sneaker he kicked twine and bits of paper off the broom-stick.

He continued his walk with the stick and machete. There was a shed deep in his woods that he wanted to check on, why, he wasn't sure.

The land Pedro worked was nearly flat in some parts, but here he was walking downhill away from his house. The shed he looked for was tiny and ancient. The roof was made of corrugated stainless steel, but the walls of the shed were indifferently put together. One side was made of *naranjo* logs he had split himself a dozen years before. Another wall was patched with large, flattened cracker cans that were rusting through. The structure had no door or windows, just some shelves that he hadn't even put to use until only recently. As he neared the shed, he heard voices and stopped in his tracks.

He couldn't make out what was being said, but he could tell the voices belonged to angry men, and he knew exactly why they were angry. He decided to confront them, though he knew this would not help matters. They were angry with him, maybe angry enough to kill him, but he shook that thought out of his mind. They might kill him, but really that shouldn't keep him from telling them what he thought, talking to them like a man, like he should have done the very first day he met them. In a few more steps, he was at the entrance to the shed.

There were two men in the shed. One of them held a gun in his hand, and his arms were crossed. The other wore shades. The one with the gun spoke first.

"Ah, so there you are. We were just about to go knock on your door. Do you mind explaining to me where everything is?" He waved the gun as he spoke, but his tone was reasonable given the circumstance, so Pedro felt comfortable telling the truth.

"I burned it."

The man raised an eyebrow and tapped his chin with the barrel of the gun. He smiled.

"Say that again?" he said. "I think I heard a very bad answer. Where's the stuff?"

"You heard me correctly. I burned it." Pedro took the matches he was carrying out of his back pocket and rattled the box.

The man lunged at Pedro as though he were about to smack him with the gun, but Pedro raised the machete so the point was an inch from the man's neck. He backed down.

The man raised his hands and smiled.

"We left twenty-four kilos. Twenty-four packages. You burned everything?"

"Everything."

"Did you burn the money?

"What money?"

"That's the wrong answer." The man pulled on the slide of his gun and aimed for Pedro's torso.

"The money I left. I took what was mine. The deal was for five thousand for a month; it has been almost two months so I took ten. I left the rest."

The man laughed softly and looked at his partner incredulously.

"Can you believe this *pendejo*? Look, Pablo . . ."

"Pedro."

"Uh-huh. Look. I'm going to explain a few things to you because I don't want you to die an idiot. First of all, when you make a contract with us, the contract is over when we say, not whenever you think. Second, you don't take the money, we give it when we're done. And third, between the kilos and the money we are missing more than a million dollars. That, we don't forgive. So I have to kill you, okay?"

"I didn't take the money," Pedro said. He kept the machete raised as though he were in an even standoff.

"Do I have your word of honor on that, Pedro?"

"Sure."

"Oh, well that makes all the difference," the man said and then he shot Pedro in the left thigh. Pedro's leg gave out under him, and he fell back and on his side, his mouth open in a silent scream and his hands, empty now, balled into fists.

"You think this is bad?" the man asked. "The day is just beginning to get bad for you, Pedro."

"Bring him," the gunman told his companion.

They dragged Pedro to a spot about ten yards behind the shed, the spot where he had burned the cocaine he had been storing for them.

"You see this pile, Pedro? We might be able to collect a kilo of product from this pile. Probably not. You were pretty thorough burning what didn't belong to you. See that bag over there?" The man pointed to a gym bag about ten feet away from where Pedro was crumpled and crying on the red clay earth of his land.

"That bag was full of money, Pedro, but you were pretty thorough there, too. Can you give me back the money, Pedro?" The man grabbed Pedro by the hair and forced him to look up.

"All I need is the money, Pedro, and then your troubles end here and now, you understand?"

"I told you, I didn't take the money."

The man put the gun to Pedro's head.

"You mean, the bag walked here by itself and emptied itself out? That would be strange."

"I don't know what happened to the money. Maybe somebody else took it . . ."

"Oh, I see. I guess I could believe that if I wanted to, but I don't want to. I want the money."

"I have ten thousand in the bank. I can get that for you right now if you want . . ."

The man tsk–tsked and shook his head.

"I want a bag full of hundreds of thousands. Can you do that for me?"

"I told you . . ."

"Yes, I know. I heard you." And the man shot Pedro's other thigh. This time Pedro screamed. He hoped someone heard him. The man with the gun crouched beside him.

"What I want to know is why, Pedro? Why? Why burn some-

5

thing that didn't belong to you? Stealing money I understand, but why burn the stuff? That doesn't make sense to me."

"Because I was ashamed," Pedro said, his face contorted with pain, neck veins bulging. "Because I should have told you to go to hell when you first showed up."

"Hmm. That's an honest answer at least. But don't worry, Pedro, we're going to hell right now. Tie him up nice and tight. Gag him."

The man's assistant took off Pedro's belt and tied his hands together; then he took off his own belt and gagged Pedro's mouth open. The gunman started walking toward Pedro's home and waved on his assistant, who dragged Pedro through the woods by his hands.

CHAPTER ONE

Luis Gonzalo, the sheriff of Angustias, sat on the edge of his bed and pulled on a sock. He stopped at midtug, seeing his reflection in the mirror in front of him. He was dressed in his best uniform, neatly starched and ironed by his wife, Mari, the night before. On his chest were several ribbons and four pinned medals—ornaments he rarely wore. Gonzalo picked at one of the medals given to him for valor and thought it ironic. That particular medal had been awarded to him by the governor of Puerto Rico after a gunfight in which Gonzalo had defended the life of Rafael Ruiz, a grocery store owner, putting down three bad guys in the process. Ruiz had had his left hand blown cleanly off his arm by a sadistic gunman that night, and though things might have gone much worse, Gonzalo could only ever think of how things could have gone better.

"What are you staring at?" his wife asked, snapping him out of his stupor. She stood in the bedroom doorway in a black dress that set off both the light brown of her skin and the curves of her figure.

"Am I just as handsome as I was twenty-five years ago?" Gonzalo asked.

Mari laughed and walked away.

"We're going to be late," she tossed over her shoulder.

Gonzalo finished dressing, then looked at himself more closely in the mirror. He was not as handsome as he had been. His mustache was flecked with gray, and his teeth had grown a bit long. The gray in his head of hair was no longer confined politely to his temples, and he no longer needed to squint or smile to show wrinkles around his eyes to go with the shadows under them that used to dissipate when he rested but were now a permanent fixture. Examining himself objectively, Gonzalo noted that he could not be said to have a proper double chin, but then neither could he call the fat beneath his chin baby fat. He made a mental note that he should start exercising again, but then scratched it out to save himself the disappointment of failing to keep to a regimen later.

And there were scars. He had worn a small scar at his chin since childhood, but there were others now. One ran for about an inch above his right eyebrow. Another was as long but Y-shaped on his left cheekbone, a gift from a local drunk who didn't want to be told he'd had enough to drink. He moved his hand to one of his more recent scars—a jagged one in his scalp at the back of his head that had taken eight stitches to close. He thought for a moment about the amount of blood he had dripped to the ground of Angustias since accepting the position of sheriff a quarter century before. A pint at least. This brought him to the worst day he had suffered as the sheriff of the small town—a day two years earlier when a set of very bad men had come to town looking for trouble. They had found it. In ten minutes they killed several citizens of Angustias, *Angustiados,* and one of his deputies. They wounded three other officers, himself included, and attacked his wife. He had never wanted to murder someone as desperately as he did on that day.

"Are you still at that mirror? *¡Caramba!* You're not a teenage girl, Luis. Get moving."

Mari stood in the doorway again, her hands on her hips, and Gonzalo wanted to hold her and clasp her face between his hands and kiss the scars she now carried from that day, but he knew they were barely visible now and no source of pride to her, and she would have found the gesture silly, so he refrained.

"I'm coming," he said. Then he finished dressing, gave his uniform a final look, and followed his wife out to the car.

The drive from the Gonzalo residence to the center of Angustias would have been only a mile or two had there been a straight road, but straight roads are in short supply in the tropical island of Puerto Rico. Nowhere are they less likely to be found than in the towns of the central mountain range. The modern traveler may think the engineers who mapped out the roads were a bit perverse, but the mapping was usually done long before any engineers showed up. Many of the roads grew up along footpaths or horse trails and these necessarily followed closely the natural contours of the earth. The routes are either scenic or challenging depending on the mood of the driver. Today Gonzalo thought of the road as challenging, not wanting to apply his mind to the ceremony he was about to attend in his own honor or the words he would be asked to say. He had thought of both these things too often for his own good already, and he could not think of a good way to say that he would have been happier if the town had let him celebrate at home or if he had been allowed to go on vacation a day earlier.

Like most ceremonies of note, the celebration for Gonzalo's twenty-five years of service was held in the town's plaza. Unlike other, larger cities, Angustias still used the plaza built by the founders more than two centuries earlier. Like many original plazas, it was situated at the heart of the city with the Roman Catholic church standing at one end and the *alcaldia* or city hall standing at the other. The homes of the wealthy had lined the sides but many of these had fallen into disrepair after having been passed down or sold to people who lacked the income of their predecessors.

The plaza was lined with trees that baked in the sun and threatened to die each summer only to be saved by a thunderstorm or two. Beneath these trees were stone benches often empty because the trees gave little shade. A fountain spurted water into the air when the water pressure sufficed. At other times it trickled pathetically until someone had mercy on it and shut it down.

On this day, as on many previous, the mayor and his deputy had called the prominent people of Angustias to the plaza—there was no other place within the limits of the town that would hold so many. When Gonzalo made it into town, he drove first to the station house attached to the rear of the *alcaldia*—like a boil was the running joke. There really wasn't anything for him to do, but there was a prisoner in custody waiting for transport to San Juan, and Gonzalo wanted to make sure there was nothing to worry about on that count. This, at least, was what he told himself. Greater honesty might have revealed a strong desire to avoid the ceremony altogether.

He walked to his desk and checked the fax and answering machines, gadgets he was still uncomfortable with. He usually let one of his younger deputies handle them. The fax machine had no paper hanging from it, which he took to be a good sign, but he made a mental note to tell a deputy that the answering machine had a light blinking on it.

"Hey sheriff," the prisoner called from his cell at the back of the precinct. "When are we leaving for San Juan?"

"It's Friday, Carlos. You're here until Monday morning, you know that."

"That's too long. I didn't do nothing wrong. Send me home already."

Carlos sat at the edge of his cot holding his head in both hands, passing them through his hair. He was one of those who had gone through school as the class clown, and his antics were simply no longer funny when committed by a man of thirty-five.

"You were drunk and disorderly at six A.M."

"I did nothing wrong. . . ."

"You punched one of my officers. I'm going to ask the judge to throw the book at you, Carlos. You used to be funny, but now you're just a joke."

"You just got no sense of humor, Gonzalo." Carlos waved Gonzalo off.

"Yeah, I guess you're right. I should have let Iris pound your brains in with her nightstick; that would have been a real laugh."

"Don't you have someplace to go, Sheriff?" Carlos asked, then laughed softly to himself and lay down on the cot again.

Gonzalo would have liked to continue the pointless conversation, but he thought better of it and decided to face the day.

The sky was nearly empty of cloud cover and with the sun shining brightly, the temperature promised to be uncomfortable. Gonzalo calculated the crowd gathered in the plaza to be numbered at about three hundred; many more were on the balconies of the houses around the plaza and finding shade in the adjacent side streets.

The new mayor was at a portable lectern near the fountain. The deputy mayor was at his side and Gonzalo's senior deputies, Hector Pareda and Iris Calderon, were standing behind them. The mayor waved for Gonzalo to make his way to him. Francisco Primavera had been in office less than a year, but he had already managed to rub Gonzalo and many others who worked for Angustias the wrong way. Rafael Ramirez, who had long been the mayor, was abrasive, loud, and demanding, but everyone knew he had the best interests of his neighbors at heart. Francisco was young and flashy, Gonzalo thought, and though he had the college degree Ramirez had never even tried to attain, it seemed that every new policy had no deeper reason than to make the new mayor look good. Gonzalo would shake his hand today, and thank him for kind words today, but he seriously contemplated retiring. He thought of this as he moved around the crowd and toward the mayor's side.

The mayor started to speak before Gonzalo took his place.

"Wow, what an honor," he said. "Twenty-five years. I was eight, Luis, when you started working here. Wow." The mayor turned to face the sheriff and started clapping. Few in the crowd followed his lead. Gonzalo raised his hand to the crowd and smiled weakly.

"Well, Luis," the mayor continued. "You deserve all the honor and praise we can bestow upon you because, wow, I mean . . ."

Gonzalo tuned out the rest of what the mayor had to say, a skill he had begun perfecting almost from the time Francisco took office. Instead he searched the faces assembled before him. In the front row was his first deputy, Emilio Collazo. Emilio was seventy-nine now and had retired only two years before after watching his partner die in a shoot-out. Collazo's rightful place was at Gonzalo's side, and the sheriff was half tempted to wave him over, but he knew his friend to be nothing if not a private man. He was content to see Collazo was still tall and strong and showed no sign of stooping to age. Collazo made a small wave and used the same hand to correct a wisp of white hair that had been blown out of place.

Rafael Ramirez was also in the front row of the crowd, standing next to his former deputy mayor, Jorge Nuñez. Ramirez was only an inch or two above five feet in height, but massively built so that he had trouble getting his arms to cross. Though Ramirez had butted heads with the sheriff on more occasions than either could count,

Gonzalo would have liked to have him at his side. In fact, as he continued to ignore the current mayor's speech, Gonzalo reflected on all the many who had helped get him through the twenty-five years that were being celebrated. He began with Mari's support. He thought of how he would never have taken the job in the first place had it not been for her. He started to form an inventory of all the times the job had made him cry and Mari had been the only one to witness his tears, but he left that to think of the young people he was working with now.

He turned to look at Iris Calderon and Hector Pareda. Hector was leaning close to Iris that moment to hear something she had to say. He smiled and said something in turn. Gonzalo caught himself taking a page from Mari's book—he wondered for the briefest instant what would happen if Hector could grow up just enough to appreciate a young woman like Iris Calderon. True, many would have thought there was a disparity of looks. Hector was twenty-nine, tall, athletic, and handsome. More than one teenage girl had confessed to having a crush on him. Iris was good-natured, but not a true beauty unless, perhaps, one had the eye of a connoisseur and could appreciate asymmetry. She also was tall, but lanky. Still, Gonzalo thought, she was younger than Hector by several years, and might fill out a bit more as she matured. And, the sheriff reminded himself, there was no disputing that she had a captivating smile.

Gonzalo was just beginning to break this train of thought (after all, the love lives of his deputies were their business) when Lucy Aponte snapped his picture. The flashbulb caught his attention. It was a bright summer day in the tropics. She was standing a few yards to his right and looked down at her camera as though she couldn't believe she had the flash on. She fiddled with it and looked up at him again. She smiled broadly and gave him a wave and a shrug, then snapped another photo. With a camera bag strapped from right shoulder to left hip, a camera in her hands and a second one hanging free at her neck, Lucy was another reminder of the attack on Angustias. She had taken pictures the men wanted destroyed. Lucy credited Gonzalo with saving her life that day. He had *tried* to save her, Gonzalo would remind her to no avail, but she had run when necessary and hidden herself, doing more to save her own life than anyone else did. The photos she had published and the stories she had written about that day and the scandals surrounding it had found homes in major magazines and won her awards. Now she spent part of the year in Angustias, but only when she wasn't practicing the photojournalism that earned her salary. He wondered if she had taken time out of her schedule just to shoot photos of his big day. But his train of thought was derailed again. There was a disturbance in the crowd and even the mayor had stopped talking.

A fire was burning on a hillside a mile or so behind the crowd. At first the image was just of a plume of smoke rising steadily but without hurry. The people on the plaza and some on the balconies turned to watch the spectacle. Because of environmental concerns, no one was allowed to burn their garbage or burn their land clear. Soon, however, it was clear this was a much bigger fire and out of control. Flames leaped into the air, and the people on the plaza started to move, though not with any purpose yet.

Collazo said something to his wife and then moved to Gonzalo's side.

"It's Pedro Ortiz's house," he said.

"You sure?"

"Yup. His property is across from a field I used to work for Martin Mendoza the father."

Gonzalo had already started walking to his car. Collazo stayed at his side. Gonzalo could see Hector Pareda jogging to the precinct ahead of him. He knew Hector would be putting in a phone call to the nearest fire department in Naranjito. That firehouse only had one truck, but they had responded to fires in Angustias before without getting lost and they were only a few miles away so they were a safer bet than larger, farther departments.

Mari had moved quickly to get the car and was waving to her husband from the driver's seat. Both Gonzalo and Collazo got in.

"It's Pedro Ortiz's house," Collazo told Mari, and she accelerated around pedestrian traffic toward the open road.

The Ortiz home wasn't that far from the plaza, but the road dipped into a valley and then rose again after a number of lazy turns, so the drive took a little more than five minutes even at sixty miles an hour. Because of the vegetation overhead, after leaving the plaza there was only an occasional view of the flames. Each glimpse made the fire seem fiercer, and Gonzalo worried there might not be any house left to rescue when he got there. The Naranjito firefighters might have nothing more to do than douse the embers of what Pedro Ortiz had built for his wife.

As they neared the house, they could see it was engulfed in flame from front to rear and top to bottom. They could see the small crowd of the nearest neighbors—a dozen people or so—standing in closed-mouth awe. What they did not see made their hearts sink and brought the three of them almost to tears.

CHAPTER TWO

The Ortiz home was in a remote area even for Angustias, a remote town. Pedro Ortiz's pickup truck sat outside his home, the driver's-side door opened wide. There wasn't a single member of the Ortiz household outside the house. It seemed that the family had not been able to get out.

The neighbors were standing by the barbed wire fence in front of the right side of the property, watching the flames, shielding their faces from the heat with the backs of their hands. On a branch over-hanging the house, the leaves of a mango tree had curled and blackened; a few of them were actually on fire; the branch swayed in the updraft of hot air. Gonzalo hopped out of the car even before Mari had brought it to a complete halt.

"¿Y la familia?" he asked. "And the family?"

The spectators ignored him. It was just as well. They knew as much as Gonzalo. The neighbors had rushed to the Ortiz home as soon as they first saw smoke, but in the few minutes it took to run within sight of the home, it had already become too late. The first persons on the scene would later report that the house was engulfed in flames almost instantly.

After a moment or two of watching the fire, Gonzalo saw Collazo approaching the house at a crouch, coming near to it from the protection of the woods and circling around to the back of the house. Gonzalo followed.

About ten yards behind the house, there was an old cement and cinder block water tower. The water tank was some twenty feet off the ground with a spigot at the bottom of one of the support columns. Gonzalo found his former deputy at the base of the tower, trying to untangle a hose.

"Pedro kept the tank filled?"

"I tried it, there's water."

Farther from the house there was a toolshed. The door was ajar. Gonzalo ran to it and found two black rubber buckets lying on their side. All the tools were thrown carelessly on the ground and finding a pair of pliers was not difficult. He filled one bucket at the spigot and ran it to the house.

Like most houses in rural Puerto Rico, cooking at the Ortiz home was done with propane gas provided by four-foot-tall tanks connected from outside the house. The Ortizes had two of them. Gonzalo used the bucket to douse the faucets at the top of the tanks, and then he shut off the flow of gas and used the pliers to cut the thin copper tubing that brought the gas into the house. He then knocked both tanks onto their sides and started to drag them, one by one, away from the flames. Before he had finished, Hector Pareda was near him to help.

"What's the plan, chief? The house is almost ready to collapse."

"What do you mean, 'what's the plan'? We don't give up, that's the plan."

Hector shrugged and strode to the back door. Without regard to the heat or the flames that were already licking at it, he kicked the door in though it would normally have swung out. The door came off its hinges and fell out toward Hector, who jumped back a step to avoid getting hit.

"I said we don't give up, not we get stupid," Gonzalo yelled, but Hector couldn't hear him.

The roar from the fire combined with the popping of wood and the crash of items within the home, made as the shelves beneath them gave up holding weight, was nearly deafening. Collazo came up to the two men with the hose in hand and poured a stream in through the opening where the door had been. The water hissed into white steam about as quickly as it went into the house at first, but moments later a toehold had been gained, and Collazo took a step through the threshold trying to carve out a path into the next room.

"Do you want me to try to crawl in?" Hector yelled to his sheriff, but Gonzalo appeared a bit distracted.

"I said, do you want me to try to—"

"I heard you. No. I'm thinking."

"It's a fire, Chief. Pretty simple," was Hector's reply.

"There's a stream on this property. Pedro's a farmer. There has to be a pump for irrigation. . . ."

Hector jogged away, each step showing he knew exactly where he was going.

There was a hedge about ten yards to one side of the house and beyond that a short declivity that ended in a stream Pedro harvested to help water tomato and pepper plots. A quick search revealed the location of a wooden storage compartment that held a pump with

generator and hoses. Within a minute, Hector had the pump running and a hose attached pulsing water. He grabbed the end of the
hose and ran it toward the house only to find that the hose was a
half-dozen feet shorter than was needed.

"Where the hell are the firefighters when you need them?" he
shouted to Gonzalo, and Gonzalo ran off for the toolshed again. He
came back with a length of PVC piping just long enough to run
from the irrigation hose to a side window. He and Hector inserted
the hose into the pipe, and Gonzalo took off his uniform shirt to
help hold the connection.

"Keep pressure on the joint and don't let the pipe come out of
the window. Just let the water pour in."

He ran back to the rear where Collazo was taking another step
into the house.

"You're relieved, old man. Get Calderon."

Iris Calderon was at the front of the house at that moment kicking at one of the white, metal Miami windows that had been rolled
shut. Under her direction several of the neighbors had strung
together about 250 feet of hose in order to bring water from a
house down the street. Collazo saw what she was trying to do and
went to the relief of one of the other deputies who was trying to
ensure no civilian got closer to the house. He was one of the new
deputies Collazo hadn't come to know yet, so he just tapped the
man's shoulder.

"I'll keep them back," Collazo said. "Go help Calderon."

The deputy Collazo sent was tall and strong and without thinking, he rammed his shoulder into the window. It clattered onto the
floor inside the house, but he hopped away with a yelp having blis-
tered his upper arm.

"That's why I was using my foot," Calderon pointed out, waving
away the smoke that billowed out of the opening now.

Calderon took control of the hose from the neighbor who

brought it and started spraying a strong stream of water onto the ceiling of the house and then onto a form that in the darkness of the front room looked like a body. It was on the floor and burning.

It seemed as though there was no place in the house that wasn't aflame. Several of the exposed cross beams in the ceiling snapped and hung down, still on fire. All of the furniture was alight and so was the floor. The hundreds of gallons poured in from the three sides had their effect, however, as did the lack of any more easily flammable materials, and another ten or fifteen minutes saw the fire under control. The noise level dropped considerably, and it was then that Gonzalo at the back of the structure could hear a baby crying.

The water tower was running dry; he dropped the hose, which was working at just a trickle then, and headed deeper into the house, into the heat and the smoke, walking in a crouch. When Calderon saw her boss coming toward her through the haze, she sprayed him with water, knowing that his clothes would be susceptible to catching fire themselves if he got too close to one of the remaining hot spots. Gonzalo ducked his head into the water stream to relieve himself of the oppressive heat and then continued to listen for the crying. He didn't have far to go.

In a bedroom to one side of the front room—the room, in fact, that Hector had been pouring water into—there was a body on the floor. This body had burned terribly, but most of the water Hector had poured into the room had fallen directly on it. Blackened and disfigured as the body was, Gonzalo instantly recognized it as Pedro's wife, Esmeralda. He saw also that her hands were behind her back and that her dress had been pulled up above her waist. The baby screamed out again, and Gonzalo located the child under the bed.

"Come with me, *muchachito*," Gonzalo implored the baby, recognizing it as Hernando Ortiz and trying to remember whether the child was more or less than six months of age.

Hernando lay in a puddle of sooty water, his face dirty from smoke, and though there had been fires all around him just moments before, he was shivering.

Gonzalo pulled the baby out from under the bed and carried him out of the house, going back the way he had come.

Outside, Gonzalo paused to check the child over. He was wet and dirty, but besides red and teary eyes that he kept rubbing with his fists, he was uninjured as far as the sheriff could tell. The boy would have to be taken to the local clinic soon, but Gonzalo held him close a few minutes, softly shushing into the child's hair, thankful that Hernando was far too young to remember his parents or his older sister or any of the details of this morning.

Mari came up behind her husband and was surprised to find the little survivor in his arms.

"He lived through that?" she asked. Gonzalo looked at her and shrugged. The child was still crying, and Gonzalo couldn't think of a better way of answering his wife than to let the child continue proving his existence.

"Let me take him; you'll never get him quiet the way you're holding him." She stretched out her arms.

Gonzalo surrendered the little boy with a kiss to the top of his head. He was skeptical of anyone's power to make the child forget his many discomforts, but Mari had him quieted in less than a minute.

"How come I couldn't do that?" Gonzalo asked.

"It's the breasts," Mari said, then she turned and started walking toward the road at the front of the house.

"He needs to go to the—"

"The clinic, I know, Luis. Just get back to work."

"Don't let them—"

"Don't let them release the child out of Angustias to anyone, I know, I know."

Gonzalo admired the figure of his wife walking away for a

moment, then heard a crash inside the house that brought his attention back to the flames.

Like many in rural Puerto Rico, Pedro Ortiz had built his house himself with help from professional contractors for those things that the law prohibited him from doing himself, particularly the electrical wiring. The house was of a simple design, made almost entirely of wood, but sturdy. It sat on six cement posts that raised it off the ground and allowed rainwater to rush underneath rather than through. Gonzalo crouched to check underneath the house and found that a furniture leg showed itself through the floor near the middle. He patted Hector on the shoulder as he made his way along the side of the house toward the front. Though the idea of using the irrigation pump had worked, the connection between hose and PVC pipe had remained loose and Hector was soaked from the waist down and standing in ankle-deep red clay mud.

"Can I get someone to relieve me, here?"

"Who?" Gonzalo asked.

"Maybe one of the new guys. . . ."

Gonzalo kept walking. At the front of the house, he found Calderon still aiming water into the house from the gaping window. Her face was twisted with determination, but when he looked into the house over her shoulder there were only two or three fairly harmless fires in isolated corners she couldn't adequately reach.

"I think this is a good job for a few buckets now," he told her.

She ignored him and kept spraying and since he didn't have a bucket with him anyway, he thought it just as well.

He walked over to Collazo who was now the only person facing a crowd that had dwindled to about a dozen spectators. Lucy Aponte was inside the perimeter, clicking photos from all angles. Gonzalo wondered how much film she could possibly have.

"Who let her through?" Gonzalo asked.

Collazo shrugged.

"She's a member of the press."

"Uh-huh. Tell her not to get close to the house, and she can't sell anything, or offer it for sale until she talks with me, okay?"

"Sure thing," Collazo answered.

"I thought I had two other deputies out here. What happened?"

"The one got a few burns on his arm and the other took him over to the clinic," Collazo answered. "What do you think?"

"Murder."

"Are you sure?"

"Well, I won't be positive until I get in there, but I would bet money on it."

"That's terrible. They were nice, young people. He worked his farm well." As a man who loved his own farm, this was about the highest praise Collazo meted out.

"Don't worry. We'll get the ones who did this." Gonzalo patted the older man on the back and started to move back toward the house. "Oh, can you stay at this post for another hour or two until I get my deputies back?"

"Yup."

When he got back to Calderon's side she was ricocheting water off the ceiling to get at a final burning corner. He watched as the fire died.

"Wow, you're pretty good with that."

"Yeah. Who needs a fire department?"

"Well, we could have finished a long time ago if we had a fire truck, but it's good enough that we got it done."

Gonzalo wet his hands in the stream from the hose and pulled at the doorknob. The pull was enough to bring both the door and part of the frame off the house. He stood at the threshold as a small cloud of ash and smoke plumed out the door.

"Shut down the water," he told his deputy. "Tell Hector to stop also."

Calderon obeyed, twisting the nozzle shut on the hose, then going over to Hector to relay the request.

Alone, Gonzalo studied the room in front of him, the crime scene. There would be time to take pictures of everything later, but he wanted to sense every detail of the scene, he wanted to try to get into the minds of the killers. Or of the victims. He wasn't sure which. He had read about this passive method of investigation before, but he couldn't remember how it was supposed to go.

"What are you waiting here for?" The voice of the mayor sounded like it was coming from only a few inches behind him, and it was. "Get in there, Luis. Take pictures, measure things, do whatever it is you're supposed to do."

Gonzalo turned to face the mayor eye to eye.

"Did I ever tell you that only my wife, my friends, and my mother call me Luis?"

"Yeah. Look. I'm here to help, Luis. Just tell me what to do. I've never worked an investigation before."

The mayor took a step into the house, and Gonzalo pulled him up short, grabbing him by his upper arm.

"What's the big idea? I'm the mayor here."

"You're in nice clothes, Mr. Mayor. If you go in there, you will never get the smell of smoke out of them."

"Oh."

"It would be best if you waited for my phone call in your office or at your house."

"What phone call?"

"I have to poke around and figure out whether this was a terrible accident or a murder. If it's an accident, I'll ask you to call the morgue. If it's murder, I'll ask you to call the *Metropolitanos.*"

"I thought you would handle the investigation."

Gonzalo walked the mayor away from the house by the elbow.

"I would. I might. I do have plane tickets for tomorrow, but let

25

me first figure out if there is even going to be an investigation. Possibly, there's no need."

"I'll be in my office then."

"Sounds fine. I'll call you within the hour."

With the mayor gone, Gonzalo was able to think clearly and he knew that he wanted to get into the mind of the killers. He surveyed the room. Near the middle of the front room lay the bound and burned body of Pedro Ortiz. The face was slightly marred by the fire but still easily recognizable. His hands were tied behind his back; his legs were splayed as though he had died kicking.

In a corner of the same room, maybe ten feet from her father, was the body of Pedro's daughter; her name escaped the sheriff at the moment. Her hands were also tied behind her back, and a patch of her hair had burned away, but her face was mostly preserved—perhaps because, unlike Pedro, she was facedown.

He stepped over to her and checked for a pulse. He was surprised to find one, faint, but there. He yelled for Hector, who rushed in. Gonzalo had already untied her hands and turned the girl over.

"She's not dead," he said. "Not yet."

He used his thumb to open one of her eyes, but he wasn't sure what sign he was looking for. He dipped his head close to her nose and mouth. There was breathing. The two men, not wanting to waste time and having no equipment that could help them, carried the girl gingerly between them out to Hector's squad car. Hector carrying the legs, Gonzalo holding on to the torso, her arms dangling free and lifeless. Lucy Aponte rushed over, snapping several photos.

"Open the door to the backseat," Gonzalo barked at her and she obeyed.

"You know what to do, Hector. I want you back here in five minutes."

Gonzalo watched as Hector pulled out, sirens blaring and lights flashing. The car was lost around a slight turn. Lucy was also looking after the car, and Gonzalo jabbed a finger in her direction.

"Collazo spoke to you?" he asked.

"I know the rules," Lucy answered.

"Follow them."

He went back into the house and tried to reorient himself.

He didn't bother just then to have a second look at Esmeralda. He remembered too clearly her general position and her burns.

Iris came in with a camera.

"Where would you like me to start?" she asked.

"Take your pick."

Iris started with varying views of Pedro and then his wife. In all the while, Gonzalo did not move from his position. He had chosen a spot where he could see each of the bodies by just turning his head and that's what he did while Iris finished shooting two rolls of film.

"So what do you think, chief?"

"I think the guys who did this were angry."

"That's it?"

"Very angry. That, and I think I have a hell of a job in front of me."

"You want me to call the mayor?"

"Not really, but do it anyway. Tell him to call the *Metropolitanos*. Have him say that there are at least two very bad men out there, armed, dangerous, and cold-blooded. But tell him not to speak to the press."

"Why not?"

"These guys are sending a message. I'd rather not pass it along just yet."

"Got it."

Iris turned to go, and Gonzalo stopped her.

"Stay a minute."

CHAPTER THREE

Gonzalo saw himself primarily as a thinking man. He enjoyed the challenge of a puzzle, and twenty-five years before when he first took the job as sheriff, he had visions of solving criminal riddles that others had abandoned as hopeless, of matching wits with masterminds. His years of service had taught him that for the most part this was the stuff of fiction. Criminals were not usually geniuses, and crimes were usually solved by following routine, by asking the right questions of the right people in the right order.

In fact, in his years as sheriff, most crimes in Angustias had revolved around missing livestock or barroom fistfights. Because of this, there were times when Gonzalo had wished for something more to do, something greater. Occasionally, Mari would find him with a distant look on his face and she would leave him to his reverie. Several times, early in their marriage, she had asked him what he was thinking, and he was always either going over the details of some forgotten crime that had baffled the FBI and Scotland Yard, or he was wishing himself in New York City or at least San Juan, places where he could make a difference.

"I wasn't born for this, Mari," he would say. "I wasn't born to figure out who stole the chicken or who hit who first in a brawl. It can't be that I'm supposed to spend the rest of my life doing this work that anyone could do, work that a monkey could do."

Mari never knew what to say to this. It was the job he chose, he was good at it, the people liked him, and the town needed him. She was sure not everyone could do the job as well as he did it; she was positive it was no job for a monkey. But none of this would help her husband, and she was sure of that, too. He knew all these things, but they didn't make the difference he was looking for.

Then came the murders. There had been several in his years as sheriff. Just two years earlier, men had come to Angustias and killed an unarmed bank guard and two innocent bystanders. They shot Collazo and Calderon and even Gonzalo himself, and they killed Rosa Almodovar, one of his deputies. That was a black day and still fresh in his memory. Perhaps darker in his mind was his first homicide case. Within months of taking the position, a young girl, a toddler, had gone missing. Gonzalo had mobilized the entire town to search for her, and hours later she was found, but it was too late. She had been raped and she had been sodomized and her internal bleeding could not be stopped. He held her while her life seeped away, and he cried. This was the one unsolved case in his career that gnawed at him, the only unsolved murder in his files.

The murders humbled Gonzalo. Or perhaps it is better to say that they chastened him. When they happened, he recognized that they were the cases he had wished for and that they were terrible things. He repented then, but it was always too late—when confronted by the lifeless eyes and the broken body, his stomach knotted and he wished the case were another barroom brawl or another stolen hen.

Gonzalo had never known Pedro Ortiz very well. Twenty-five years earlier, Pedro had been a grade-schooler. Gonzalo had watched over him and the other children as they got on and off the school bus, but after high school, Pedro had worked his father's farm, and then a few years later he inherited it. He had married a woman from the next town over, Esmeralda, and together they lived quietly and raised a family. Too quietly, Gonzalo thought now. If only he had gotten into a little trouble, Gonzalo would have a record of him, would have had reason to keep an eye on him. The murders would not have come as such a big surprise then. It was now that Gonzalo truly understood that he had not known Pedro Ortiz at all.

"Whatcha thinking, boss?" Calderon asked.

Gonzalo paused a moment before answering; he pondered whether the truth would at all be instructive or helpful.

"I was thinking that I hardly knew this family, and if I had paid just a little more attention, they would probably be here now enjoying the day."

"Well, you're paid to deal with the troublemakers," Calderon tried.

"Yeah. I told myself that already. Anyway. No difference now. What I don't know isn't going to help me solve this case."

"Shouldn't we call the *Metropolitanos*?"

Los Metropolitanos were the police branch of Puerto Rico that patrolled the larger cities and had the resources to assist on big cases in the smaller towns. They had the labs, the homicide division detectives, and the prestige, but they were technically of equal rank with the rest of the police on the island. All worked for the state government though *Los Metropolitanos* wore blue and *Los Gandules*, the pigeon peas, wore green. The officers in green, like Gonzalo, did most of the highway patrol and guarded the small towns. They lacked the respect afforded to their brothers in blue though they carried guns and badges, enforced the same laws, and bled and died just like *Los Metropolitanos.*

"Sure. This crime scene is a mess already; it's more than we can handle on our own." Gonzalo sounded apologetic.

"I understand, boss. Fire and water; even *Los Metropolitanos* are going to have a hard time collecting evidence here."

Calderon paused a moment. In her two years of service, she had not seen Gonzalo look so utterly overwhelmed as he did then. She reminded herself that he had already had a terrible day and it wasn't noon yet, but the sight still scared her a little.

"What do you think happened here?"

"Well," Gonzalo started. "We'll need to get autopsies, but the basics are clear."

He moved close to Pedro and motioned for Calderon to join him as he squatted at the dead man's feet. He pointed with his pinky.

"Pedro was caught outside. See the burr stuck to what's left of his pant leg? See the little coffee bean caught in the laces of his sneaker? In fact, see the mud on the soles here? I don't think Esmeralda would have let him in the house that way. No self-respecting housewife would. There is mud on his shoulders and on the hands. Also, here and here."

"He was dragged?" Calderon asked.

"Yup. This suggests that the bullet wounds to his legs, here and here"—he pointed out the holes in the one remaining pant leg and the hole in the thigh where the pant had burned away—"these wounds were probably done out on the farm somewhere."

"What kind of a murderer shoots people in the woods, then brings them home like this?"

"Good question. There's a partial answer in the bedroom."

Calderon turned to look into the bedroom Gonzalo pointed out;

she could see among the mess of clothes and bureau top items the burned body of Esmeralda, partially disrobed.

"A rapist?"

"Maybe, but look at the bureau."

All the drawers of the bureau had been pulled out most of the way and emptied onto the floor.

"Someone who's looking for something."

"Right. What, I don't know, but obviously it was something that could fit into a bureau drawer. The door is open on Pedro's truck, so I assume they searched it also. There might be some prints we can use there."

Hector walked into the house again.

"Doctor Perez says Jessica's in a coma," he said.

"Will she make it?"

Hector shrugged, and the look on his face told Gonzalo the doctor had given him no encouragement.

"It's a shame," Hector continued. "She's a sweet little girl."

"You knew her?" Gonzalo asked.

"She's afraid to cross the street alone. I walk her in the afternoon to get her on the schoolbus . . ."

Iris interrupted him with a laugh.

"What's so funny?"

"She's not afraid to cross the street, Hector. She wants to hold your hand. She has a crush on you."

"Nonsense."

Gonzalo smiled at his deputies, but brought them back to the reality of the case in front of them before Calderon could start singing "Hector's got a girlfriend."

"We need to call in the *Metropolitanos*. This case is a little more than we can handle."

"I would agree with you," Hector said. "But isn't there a workers' rally today?"

"He's right," Calderon said. "The people from the *telefonica* should be in the streets right about now. I'll bet every *Metropolitano* in San Juan is in riot gear. The detectives are all probably working the cut phone line cases or they're pulling a second shift patrolling the streets. You may need to go without them." Of course, this was what she was hoping for. In her mind, there was no need for the *Metropolitanos* to get the glory when the Angustias precinct could handle the job.

"Maybe," Gonzalo said. He had gone back to examining Pedro; now it was the head that interested him. He put his own head close to the water on the floor and searched the scalp intently.

"What's so interesting, chief?" Hector asked.

"Nothing."

"Then why are you looking so hard?"

"I mean that what is interesting is the fact that I don't find a bullet wound in the head. The other two were both shot in the head, Esmeralda in the temple, and I think they were trying to get Jessica straight in the back of the head, but it looked like the bullet grazed her skull, maybe fractured it. That bullet's probably buried in the mud under this house."

"What does it mean?" Calderon asked.

"I think it means that Pedro was left to burn alive, but the killers had some mercy on the other two."

"What makes you so sure there was more than one killer?" It was Hector's turn to ask.

"I think one person could easily kill three others, but it isn't so easy to tie them up. For instance, who would hold his gun while he tied up the girl? And if he puts his gun away, even in his waistband, how is he going to keep people from fighting him and running away? He had help. I just don't know how much."

"So what's the scenario so far, boss?" Calderon asked. It was clear from her wrinkled brow that she was putting the pieces of the puzzle together in her own mind.

"Well, one hates to jump to conclusions in any kind of case, and there is a hell of a lot of evidence to collect, but I think he was wounded outside, dragged here. Esmeralda saw the trouble that was coming to her door and she hid the baby under the bed. Maybe she hid the older child, too, but she was at that age where a child can't stay quiet when there's trouble. The guys came in, they searched the place, they roughed up Esmeralda and then killed her and set fire to the place. Gasoline. Pedro dies in the fire."

Calderon put her nose up into the air sniffing. The air was acrid with the smoke.

"You smell gasoline, boss?" she asked.

He pointed at a gallon-sized gasoline can lying on its side in a corner. It was blackened, but the nozzle to it marked it clearly enough.

"How long before we noticed the fire?" Hector asked. He also was thinking through the evidence.

"Hard to say. I figure it couldn't have been burning more than five minutes before people in the plaza started to notice. It took us another five or six minutes to get here. We found out it was murder after fighting the fire for about . . . twenty minutes?"

"I think more like thirty," Hector put in and Calderon agreed.

"Okay, thirty minutes—"

"That means the killers could be anywhere on this island by now," Calderon said.

"Or they could still be around. Or they'll be back," Gonzalo answered.

"The killer always returns to the scene of the crime?" Calderon asked.

"That's a myth. If they think what they were looking for is still

here, they'll be back. The guys who did this weren't very sentimen-
tal. They're not going to be back just because this is where they
killed a family. If they come back, it'll be because they left something behind."

"Why would they burn the place down if they thought what
they wanted was still here?"

"They may not come back to this house, Calderon; obviously
what they want is no longer here. But it might be somewhere in
Angustias or even on this farm."

"Or they might have it already."

"Yup. Let's not worry about that. We don't even know what they
wanted."

"What did the Ortiz family have?"

Hector answered, "Not much. The deed to this property, the
truck that's still parked outside, some tools, and all the yams, bananas,
coffee, and avocados you could ever want."

"Right," Gonzalo said sharply as though trying to wake himself
from a daze. "Let's get started. Hector, dust the truck outside for
prints. Do the shed out back, too. They seemed to have gone
through it, so give it a shot. Calderon, get Collazo to help you out
on the farm. Find me where Pedro was shot and the blood trail he
made when he was dragged here."

"Collazo? Boss, he's not on the payroll anymore."

"We'll work something out; he knows every farm in Angustias
like you know your own house. Besides, he needs the exercise."

Hector started for his squad car. Calderon asked another question.

"What are you going to be doing?"

"I have a bunch of people I need to talk to, and I'm going to start
with a call to Primavera, then a trip to the clinic. I'll check on
Jimenez there and see if I can't get him and Ramos back in the
field." Gonzalo took out a pen and a small notepad from his gun

belt. "I'll also make the call to the medical examiner in Ponce." He jotted something down and went out the front door to his car.

The ride to the only medical facility in Angustias was a short one from the Ortiz home, so Gonzalo tried to clear his mind for the few minutes it would take to get there. There was no point in trying to drive and think through the case at the same time. Instead, he thought of the fact that this crisis had shown him all too clearly that he couldn't really work with the new mayor. Everything about the man rubbed him the wrong way. More importantly, in a chaotic moment, the mayor must know what to do to calm the situation, not make things worse. Ramirez had never been the best at this, but the new guy was terrible. He didn't know the first step. Gonzalo knew he was being unfair. Ramirez had learned his job during three terms of office; still, he just didn't have the patience to help the new guy learn. He wanted to quit, he told himself. Or maybe he could just talk to the mayor and straighten a few things out. In any event, he was at the clinic and there was a case to work right now. These issues would have to wait.

As he pulled into the clinic parking lot, he didn't notice the open black Jeep that had followed his car. It was new and the type of car the hoodlums from the big cities were making popular with wannabe gangsters. He slowed as he turned off the road, and both the driver and passenger took a good look at him. Then they sped up, went round a bend in the road, made a U-turn, and went past the clinic again toward the Ortiz property. Gonzalo was getting out of his car by then and looked up at the car as it passed. He could have sworn someone in the car waved, but he shrugged off the thought and went inside.

CHAPTER FOUR

In his office in the *alcaldia* Francisco Primavera was on the phone with a sergeant of the Mayagüez *Metropolitanos*. This was hardly the nearest unit, but three other units had refused to send anyone out. Besides having to deal with large groups of strikers from the phone company and sympathizing unions, and investigating damage to phone lines that the governor had made top priority, the *Metropolitanos* were handling an ongoing hostage situation and the normal number of assaults and robberies around the island. One police officer had asked why it was that hicks could never take care of their own troubles. Another had clearly been talking to at least one other person while handling Primavera's call and slammed down the receiver, saying that they didn't handle fires.

"We need a homicide detective here," Primavera was sputtering into the phone. He had already been told that there wasn't one in the station house.

"You're from Angustias?" The sergeant was practically yawning as he asked.

"Yes, we're a small town. We only have five police officers and none of them is a detective so—"

"But don't you guys have . . . what's his name? Gonzalez, Luis Gonzalez over there, or did he retire?"

"Luis Gonzalo is the sheriff here, but he's not a—"

"Then believe me, Mr. Mayor, you don't need us. Gonzalo knows what to do. Tell him to give us a call if he gets stuck. Other than that, all I can say is that we might be able to send someone over by tomorrow morning, but not before that."

The sergeant hung up the phone without bothering to say good-bye, and Primavera rolled his eyes as he put the receiver back in place.

The door opened and Rafael Ramirez peeked into the office. Ramirez had never been known for his delicacy, but he seemed to feel out of place in the office that had been his for a dozen years. He stood near the door and looked around the room, though he'd been in it several times since losing the last election to the much younger man. He had been upset at first at all the changes Primavera had instituted—moving the desk, buying new flags even though the old ones were not that badly worn. On this occasion, Ramirez took a quick look around the room before approaching his successor. He noticed that the picture of the governor had been moved.

"Is there anything I can help you with?" Primavera said with a voice that added, "I'm very busy, Ramirez, so make it short."

"It was murder, right?"

"Yes. That much I can tell you. It was definitely murder. But again, is there anything I can do to help you?"

"Actually, Primavera, I'm here to see if you need my help. There were a few serious crimes in my time as mayor, so I thought that maybe . . ."

"If you can get a homicide detective to come to Angustias, the town would be in your debt." Primavera was curt with the former mayor. Whenever they spoke, it always seemed that he could not stop seeing the older man as an opponent.

"What's wrong with Gonzalo?" Ramirez asked.

"Gonzalo's fine, but he's not a homicide detective, is he?"

"I don't know about that. I think if there is anyone on the island who can figure out who did this it would be him."

"Yes, I've heard that he is very smart, and in a normal case, I would certainly trust him, but this might be a little more than he can handle. . . ."

"If that's the case, then there's no one who can handle it. Believe me, Gonzalo can catch the men you want."

"He himself asked me to call for the *Metropolitanos*. He knows he needs help."

"I wouldn't be too sure. Maybe he just wanted you to stay out of his way. Even if *Los Metropolitanos* wanted to get up here, they wouldn't be here for hours. Why, one time the FBI wanted to butt in on a case, and even they couldn't find this town. Not too many people know we're here. Most of the time, all we have is each other."

"Tell me about it," Primavera muttered to himself. "Look, why don't you ask Gonzalo if he needs any of your help?"

Ramirez made a short, quick bow and exited the room. In the hallway, he met up with Jorge Nuñez, his former deputy mayor.

"Murder?" Jorge asked.

"Of course."

The pair walked down the hallway toward the exit. Jorge was tall and thin with dark skin and hair that was slicked back into something like a pompadour. Ramirez was squat and round so that his arms seemed to stick out like the handles of a sugar bowl.

"Is Gonzalo on the case?"

"No. We've got to go find him. That fool in there is trying to take Gonzalo off the case. He wants *Los Metropolitanos* to take over."

Jorge smiled to himself. In his years as mayor, Ramirez had often doubted Gonzalo's ability to hunt down criminals. And he had often called in the city police even though, as Ramirez had told the current mayor, they usually had a hard time finding Angustias and arrived hours late or sometimes not at all. The two men stepped out into the sunlight of the plaza.

"What are you smiling at?" Ramirez asked.

"Nothing. Don't you hear that?"

Ramirez paused. In the distance there was the sound of a siren. The fire truck had finally arrived somewhere near town. In fact, both men could tell the truck was heading straight for the center of town. They took a bench on the plaza under a tree that did nothing to keep the waxing sun off them and waited for the firefighters to come to them asking directions.

Back at the Ortiz property, Iris Calderon and Emilio Collazo were walking through the backyard and heading to the farm; Calderon brought along a small camera, which she squeezed into a shirt pocket. The blood trail had been easy to spot and the only difficulty in following it into the woods was likely to be the rugged terrain. Pedro Ortiz owned nearly forty acres, and the area that the trail went into was a section that hadn't been cleared off for planting. It didn't need as much attention because it was dense with fruit trees that took less care than low-growing plants like tomatoes and peppers.

The land here began with a sharp decline that Calderon found a little daunting. It was easy to lose one's footing on the red clay earth; it needed only a little moisture to become as slippery as an oil slick, and water from the house had begun to trickle down the hill in several places. Besides, she had just come from the puddles inside the house.

Though he was nearly eighty years of age, Collazo was able to maneuver through the woods without a pause. Within a minute, he had opened a wide gap between himself and the deputy.

"Hold on a minute," she called out.

Collazo stopped and turned to face Calderon who was now a hundred feet behind him.

"What happened?" he asked.

"You're going too fast. It's not easy to find a good place to put your foot here. It's very steep."

"Oh."

Iris was trying to follow in Collazo's footsteps, but his legs were longer and he was so sure of each step. He had been walking across land just like this since early boyhood, so the decision to place his foot on one root rather than another, to step onto one clump of weeds and not another was instantaneous for him. There were good reasons for each of his choices but these were lost on Iris, and she paid with a slip each time she chose to deviate from the path he was marking out for her.

Finally, Iris made it to Collazo's side.

"Did you hold on to that banana tree back there?"

"Yeah. Why?"

Collazo reached for her hair saying, "There were a few of the flying roaches in it and now there's one in your hair." He opened his hand before her eyes and showed how he had pinched a three-inch-long roach between his thumb and palm.

"Disgusting," she said.

"They like bananas and that tree has been let go. The fruit is just rotting on it."

"Why would a farmer do something like that?"

"Like what?"

"Why wouldn't Pedro pick those bananas?" It was clear Officer Calderon was trying to find some connection to the case.

"Maybe he doesn't like bananas. This type of banana isn't very sweet. It probably just grew wild."

Collazo started out again, but at a slower pace. In another minute, they came upon the spot where Pedro had destroyed the hornets' nest. Collazo crouched to look through the underbrush.

"There's a shed straight back that way." He pointed.

"Let's go check it out."

Collazo headed out at a slight angle away from the shed.

"Where are you going?"

"There's another hornets' nest. I thought we should go the long way around it."

Iris followed him, still trying to find the hornets' nest he had seen but without luck. A few steps later they were back on a direct course and on the blood trail again.

Near the door of the shed, there was a large bloodstain on the ground and flies had gathered. Calderon took a step into the shed. It had several shelves on the walls and a small table in one corner but was otherwise empty. There was, she found, a bullet casing on the mud floor. She squatted and inspected it, putting the tip of a pen into the empty shell and lifting it close to her eyes in order to read off the butt end. She put it back down where she had found it, and from her squatting position she looked around the shed, searching for the other shell she knew had to be somewhere. Collazo moved away a few steps.

"Look at this, *mi'ja*," he said, pointing at a blood trail that led farther into the forest and away from the house. The two followed it a short distance to the pile of burnt cocaine, to the empty gym bag, to another splatter of blood where Pedro had lain while his murderer spoke.

The area where Pedro had received his second wound was a small clearing with a dense canopy of leaves. It was shaded and cool there though the sun was high in the sky. There was mottled sunlight on the ground, and the area was so perfectly devoid of outside noises from the street or neighboring houses that the sound of each leaf rustled by lizards and the chatter of each bird was distinct. Surprised by what they both knew to be the remains of an enormous amount of illicit drugs on the property of a quiet farmer, Calderon and Collazo stood in silence for a moment. An overripe breadfruit falling and crashing through the branches woke them from their stupor. It took some work to even begin to make sense of the evidence before their eyes.

"Could he have grown the cocaine here, on this farm?" Calderon asked.

Collazo hesitated a moment before answering.

"That much cocaine? I think that would have taken a large field and a lot of his time and energy. I'll look over his land step by step, but I don't think he could have done that. He was bringing other fruits to market regularly."

"Right. No. I don't think so, either. It was just a thought. But then, why would it be here?"

"Just collect information. Let your boss figure it out."

Calderon did as Collazo advised, taking out her camera and photographing the wasted pile, the gym bag, the stain of blood, and several sets of footprints. She found another shell casing from its glint in a spot of sunlight on the ground and identified it as being the same type as the first casing. She left it where she found it. Gonzalo would want to see the site in as close to its original condition as possible.

There was the noise of an automatic camera from a spot behind them, and Calderon and Collazo turned to see Lucy Aponte taking photos of them and the pile of drugs.

"I thought you said you were leaving," Collazo said. He wasn't pleased by her presence at the moment though he and the young lady usually got along very well.

"I did. I got more film," she said. She snapped a few more pictures rapidly. "This story's bigger than I thought," she told no one in particular.

"How did you get past Hector?" Calderon asked. Her face showed her displeasure, and Lucy thought about taking a picture of her in angry-face, but decided against it.

"There's a lot of land," Lucy said. "And not much fencing."

"You can't sell anything without talking to Gonzalo first," Collazo reminded her. He walked toward her slowly. It was her signal that she should leave.

"I know that," she answered. "I just want to make sure I have something to sell for when he gives me the okay."

She took another half-dozen pictures in quick succession, then turned to go.

"I'll be around," she tossed over her shoulder. "Let me know if anything else comes up, okay?"

Collazo promised and watched her march back toward the house on a longer but easier route.

"We need to put up some crime scene tape," Calderon said.

"He had almost forty acres. I don't think we have enough tape for that," Collazo answered. "We need to stay at the house and make sure nobody disturbs that area."

"What do you think about the bag?" Collazo asked as they made their way back to the house.

"Well, it was too small to hold all that coke. Gonzalo said the men who did all this were looking for something. I think they thought the gym bag had what they were looking for, but it wasn't in there. They tortured Pedro and killed his family to find what was in the bag."

"Money," Collazo said.

"Well, we can't be sure it was—"

"Money, *mi'ja*. Drugs and money go hand in hand. It was money." They walked on silently a bit longer before Collazo asked another question.

"How much money do you think fits in a bag like that?"

"Who can say? Maybe a million dollars."

"Why was it here?"

"What do you mean?"

"Why was there a million dollars on Pedro's property? Why was there cocaine here? I don't think he could have grown it. Why would drug dealers bring all that money and drugs to Angustias? Why would they bring it to this farm? It doesn't make sense, does it?"

Collazo had always liked the puzzles that came with police work and he had often marveled at Gonzalo's ability to tie clues together in building a case. He had also admired Calderon's computer savvy and her inquisitive mind, and he was hoping she might be able to deduce some answer from what seemed to be the abundance of evidence they had just come across. For her part, Calderon was just finding it difficult to make her way up the hill to the house.

"I'm not sure about these things, Collazo. I do think it is better if we think of these guys as killers for now and get them off the streets. Then we can ask them personally about all these things."

"Well, they'll be back," Collazo stated firmly.

"Yeah? What makes you think so?"

"They shot Pedro, they took him to the drugs, they shot him again. By this time he knows they are very serious. They start to drag him to his house, his wife and his children. If he could have given them the money, he would have, right?"

"Sounds right."

"If he gave them the money or offered to take them to it, they would have gone to get the money, right? I mean, maybe they kill him anyway, but they don't go to the house and waste their time there if he tells them the money is hidden or buried or something like that, right?"

"Still sounds good."

"So I think he told them he didn't know where the money was and it was the truth. The only thing was that they didn't believe him. They searched the house, they tortured the family, then they killed everybody and left. Don't you think so, *mi'ja*? Sounds good, no?"

"Sounds good."

"So then the killers have no choice. They have to come back here. It's either that or give up on the money. You see what I mean?"

Iris Calderon stopped for a few seconds in her hike back to the Ortiz home and rested with the palm of one hand on her knee and the other palm on a tree trunk. She thought through the older man's argument and found that she did indeed see what he meant.

"That's some good deduction, Collazo. I think you may have just figured out a very important piece of information. Now we have some idea what to expect."

"Maybe Gonzalo can set a trap, no?"

"That might be possible."

They crested the hill and were back in the Ortizes' backyard again. Collazo stopped and waited for his younger companion to catch up. When she did, he was smiling broadly and pointing to his temple.

"What?" Calderon said, knowing he was proud of his achievement. "I never said an eighty-year-old couldn't do police work."

"Oh, I know I can still think as good as a young person; it's your hair." He reached to a lock of hair that was running down her right temple. "You picked up another of these roaches." He showed her the bug pinched between his palm and thumb, then he flung it into the air toward the woods and it took wing and flew clumsily away.

"Did you find anything useful?" Hector asked as they approached him at the front of the house. He was closing up an evidence kit, having dusted Pedro's truck and the toolshed at the back of the house.

"We found a ton of evidence, and I think Collazo has figured out a reason why the killers are probably going to come back sooner rather than later."

"Well, I never doubt the old man."

"Anything useful here?"

"Too easy. The door handles here and in the shed have several bloody prints. There's a full set of prints here on the seat. I guess the killer was looking under the seat and held himself up here. We'll fax the prints to San Juan. If this person's in the system, we should have a response in a day or two."

Calderon opened her mouth as though to say something, but Hector trained his eyes on a black Jeep that drove along the road toward town.

"That car has passed by here at least three times now. I don't know who they are, but they're beginning to bother me."

"People do get lost in Angustias all the time. . . ." Collazo said, but he and the others were all thinking that the two young men in the car were not lost at all but looking for something.

"Well, by now Gonzalo and the other two are canvassing," Hector said. "I'm going to the station house. You guys stay here and secure the scene, okay?" His nostrils were flaring, his eyes were still looking off in the direction the car had gone, and it was clear to the other two that he intended to find out something more about the young men in the Jeep.

"Don't get hurt, Hector," Calderon said softly, and to Collazo's embarrassment, the young man took a step toward her, cupped her chin in his right hand, and drew her closer. Then he kissed her, on the lips, fully and with passion. She returned his kiss and wanted to embrace him, but he stepped away, got into his squad car, and drove off to town.

CHAPTER FIVE

Two years earlier, the city of Angustias had been granted three extra officers to add to the three who had taken care of the city for several years past—Gonzalo, Hector Pareda, and Emilio Collazo. The new three included Iris Calderon, Officer Rosa Almodovar, and Officer Abel Fernandez. In one terrible day, Officer Fernandez was fired for cowardice and Officer Almodovar was killed in the line of duty. Collazo, then seventy-seven, was wounded and retired. In the time since that day, no funding had been provided for replacement of those officers. Though all admitted that Angustias had suffered a bad break when a rogue cop decided to attack the town, Angustias could not escape the stigma of having recklessly thrown away and killed perfectly good officers.

The two new officers Gonzalo was working with were on loan to Angustias from among a batch of newly graduated cadets. They would be going to their permanent posts in six weeks when they would be replaced by other recent graduates or by officers who were looking to coast a last few months to retirement. In the years since the death of Almodovar, Angustias had seen several pairs travel through the town on their way to other positions, and they had experienced long stretches when Gonzalo, Pareda, and Calderon were the only law enforcement officials assigned to the town. Often, Gonzalo preferred it this way.

When he walked into the clinic that day, both his new officers were sitting in the waiting room, flipping through magazines. The larger of the two men, Officer Pablo Jimenez, was only twenty-two years old. He had dropped out of college, had done fairly well as a cadet, and was hoping for a post in San Juan, the capital of Puerto Rico and a city of more than a million inhabitants; this is where all the action was. This, at least, was what he had told Gonzalo. When Gonzalo saw him sitting with a copy of *Sports Illustrated* in his hands, he thought the young man looked like the last person to seek out adventures. There was a small bandage on his right upper arm, and his sleeve was rolled up exposing some redness to the open air.

Neither man stood up as Gonzalo addressed them though they would have learned to do so in the academy.

"What are you guys waiting for?" Gonzalo tried to keep a positive tone of voice—after all, one of the deputies was actually injured in the line of duty.

"Dr. Perez wanted him to stick around for some antibiotics, then he said I should drive him home so he can get some rest."

The deputy who spoke was Officer Roberto Ramos. In his thirties already, Gonzalo suspected him of more than a little laziness. He had expressed an interest in working in Angustias permanently.

"We have a double homicide and it could be a few hours before we get any help on this. I'm sorry for your injuries, Jimenez, but I really need you guys out on the streets today. As soon as possible, I'll let you go home, okay?"

One of the nurses walked into the waiting room with a white bag that obviously held the anticipated prescription. Gonzalo and Officer Ramos took a step out of the room as she began giving the young officer instructions.

"A double homicide, huh? A couple of years ago it was how many that died?" Ramos started, his arms crossed.

Gonzalo studied his deputy's face for a moment and decided then and there that the man wasn't going to be a good match for Angustias. His answer to the question was brief.

"Enough."

Pablo Jimenez came out to the hallway, and the three officers walked out to the parking lot.

Gonzalo looked up to the sky. He had found long ago that the contemplation of nature helped him clear his mind of distractions and gather his thoughts. There were dark clouds in the distance. He looked around himself to find in which direction they lay, and knew the clouds would be coming over Angustias. This is one of the strange features of life in Puerto Rico: storm clouds move quickly enough to be easily studied—from a hilltop one can often tell which neighboring town is being hit with a deluge though, at the moment, one sits under a sunny sky.

"It's going to rain," Gonzalo pointed out to his deputies. They looked at the clouds and shrugged.

"What do you want us to do?" Officer Jimenez asked.

"Did you guys learn about canvassing a neighborhood? Asking questions, getting answers, and not giving information away?"

Both men nodded. Gonzalo spoke to them slowly and with care.

"Good. Then we're going to put that lesson to work. Shots were fired. There must have been yelling and screaming. There's a lot of vegetation and not that many houses around, but somebody must have heard something, seen something, and we are going to start asking questions. You guys follow me in your car, and I'll lead you to where I want you to start asking questions—'Did you hear anything? See anything? Have there been suspicious people around? People you don't know, et cetera?' I want you guys to work your way from where I leave you to the Ortiz house. Got all that?"

"Are any of these people suspects?" Ramos asked.

"Nope. All the people you'll be meeting are longtime citizens of Angustias; most of them are elderly, in fact. Treat them all with respect; hopefully they can help us do our job. Now, don't worry too much if you don't get any good information. They may not have associated loud noises with gunshots. They may not know what you mean by a suspicious person. They might be afraid to say anything. Got that? Again, respect is the key here."

The two men got into their squad car and Gonzalo into his. He led them to a graveled driveway about five hundred yards short of the Ortiz property. Like most driveways in the neighborhood, it curved and seemed to get lost in the underbrush, but Gonzalo assured his officers there was a house at the end of it.

"Doña Fela lives there. She's about eighty or ninety years old and not always perfectly in her right mind; she never was. She'll offer you soda and cookies; drink the soda, leave the cookies. I'll be up the road."

The two men drove up the driveway, but it soon became too narrow for the car, so they walked the last few dozen yards to a one-room shack settled on four concrete posts. There were chickens in the yard and a goat tied to a stump in the tall grass to the left of the house. Doña Fela, a tiny woman in a house frock, carried a metal bucket across her yard and walked into her house with it, not noticing the two officers waving to her.

"Doña Fela," Officer Ramos called out. She turned around, standing in the doorway of her house.

"Doña Fela, we need to ask you a few questions."

"The water's mine," she responded, and then she shut the door on the officers.

Neither man could figure out what her response had to do with anything. Collazo could have told them that she was referring to the water in the bucket she carried. Her family had been embroiled in a dispute over the ownership of a stream at the rear of her property; the dispute dated to a time long before she was born and nobody had thought about it in decades except for Fela, who sometimes feared the stream would be redirected away from her in the middle of the night. It was a thought that stole her sleep. The sight of the police officers on her property had made her think she might somehow be forced to give back all the water she had ever used.

"We need to ask you some questions." Ramos spoke through the door. "It's about some loud sounds." He watched her through a knot hole in the wood of the door and saw her relax her shoulders when she heard that her water was not the issue.

"The water is still mine," Doña Fela warned.

"Yes, yes. We just want to hear about the loud noises."

She opened the door and looked at both men closely, one after the other.

"The loudest noise I ever heard was when I was—"

"No, no. I mean noises today, Doña Fela, today. Did you hear anything loud today?"

Fela looked up at the sky before turning to the men with an answer.

"I heard music. Loud music."

"No, no. Like gunshots."

"Gunshots? Who did you kill?"

"Did you hear any gunshots or not, Doña Fela? It's very important that you tell us."

"You want me to say I heard gunshots?"

"Did you?"

"No. But if it's important for me to tell you that I did, then—"

"No, no. Have you seen anyone suspicious in the area?"

"Ah, yes. Don Jose across the street and up the hill. He doesn't trust anyone. He has been suspicious all of his life, and he is older than me. You should talk to him."

"No, no, Doña Fela, I mean have you seen anyone new in the area, someone you have never seen before?" Ramos continued though he could no longer tell why.

Doña Fela thought for a minute with a look on her face that showed she was debating whether she should say what was on her mind.

"Doña Fela, it is very important," Ramos tried to prod her. "If there is anyone suspicious, anyone you haven't seen before, you have to say."

"Well, I don't want to offend anyone. You see?"

"Don't worry about that," Ramos said, pulling out a pen from his shirt pocket and reaching for the notepad in his back pocket.

"Well, I've never seen you two before. Is that what you want to hear?"

The officers left Doña Fela with the halfhearted thanks of the Angustias police force and made their way back to the squad car.

On his end, Gonzalo was able to collect more information. First he drove back to the Ortiz property and got a rundown of the investigation so far from Calderon and Collazo. The news made an obvious impact on him as he absorbed it while sitting in his squad car.

"Drugs? You think you know somebody. You see them every week in church, in the stores, on the roads, then they turn out to be someone you can't even recognize."

"You can't blame yourself for that, son," Collazo offered, though he knew Gonzalo would blame himself anyway.

"No. I guess not," Gonzalo said absentmindedly. "How much did you say you found?"

Calderon gestured with her hands to indicate the approximate size of the mound that sat charred near the shed in the woods behind the Ortiz home.

"Son of a bitch," he said. Then he hit his steering wheel with the palm of his left hand while using his right to shift the car into reverse.

"What's the matter, boss?" Calderon asked.

"That much cocaine is too much for this town alone," he said as he started to back away. "That means Angustias has probably been the distribution point for the drugs hitting the other towns around here."

Gonzalo turned his car toward the Ortizes' nearest neighbor and parked in front of a home across the street and over a low rise.

Don Julio had lent the use of his garden faucet to help put out the fire and had several people still in his house. He was over eighty years of age and could usually be found sunning himself on a bench in the town's plaza. Because of the crowd that had gathered early for Gonzalo's anniversary ceremony, he had left the plaza almost as soon as he arrived, taking a *carro público*, one of several cars for hire that serviced Angustias, back home in disgust. After all, he thought to himself, he had been of service to his neighbors for many years before Gonzalo had ever drawn breath and no one gave him a medal for his efforts. Not that he harbored any animosity toward the sheriff personally. It was more the world and all the people in it that he resented. The people in his house were gladly listening to him retell the story of the fire and his role in putting it out. Gonzalo called for Don Julio to come out where he could question the man in relative peace. Don Julio was happy to comply. His guests stood in the doorway as the sheriff and Don Julio walked a few paces from the house.

"I need to ask you a few questions about the Ortiz family and the events of today," Gonzalo started.

"I always help the police whenever I can, you know that, Luisito." Don Julio used the diminutive form of Gonzalo's name, a form Gonzalo hadn't heard since childhood except from Don Julio and a few of the other older residents of Angustias.

"Yes, well, I wonder if you heard the shots, for instance."

"They were shot? No. I can't say I heard any shots. I don't hear much up here. I'm more than eighty years old and my hearing, well, you can imagine. . . ."

"Yes, okay. Then I wonder if you have seen anyone suspicious around here."

"Well, you can talk to Don Jose across the street and down the road, he's been suspicious of people . . ."

"No, I mean has there been anyone new in the area, people who visit the Ortiz family, people who maybe park outside their home . . ."

"*Ah, ya veo.* Yes, of course, there have been suspicious people, more than one and several times." The old man adjusted his glasses and folded his arms across his chest and looked up into the woods behind his house.

"Can you tell me about these people?" Gonzalo hated having to pull teeth, but he knew Don Julio would try to play the moment for all it was worth. "The people of Angustias really need your help on this matter, Don Julio. There might be killers out on the loose. I'm sure the governor himself would be grateful to you for this service."

"Okay, it's like this. Two men, young, with short hair, one dark skin, one light skin, in a Jeep. A black Jeep. I have only seen them from far, so I don't know if they are tall or short, but they are both young, ah, and they have muscles; they wear the shirts that let you see the muscles." Don Julio stopped talking and recrossed his arms.

"When have you seen them?"

"Two or three times in the last few months. Two times they parked in front of the house and went into the property. They don't stay too long. You know why I remember them?" The old man beamed into Gonzalo's face.

"Why do you remember them, Don Julio?"

"Because I remember that whenever they show up and go into the property, the Ortiz family is not there. They are not visiting the family, they are visiting the land. I figure they know Pedro Ortiz and maybe they are looking to buy a piece of land from him. But then, I say, *caramba*, maybe they are stealing fruits. You know how kids are nowadays, *sin vergüenzas*. But I talked to Pedro and he said it was all right, they just work for him. He has a few men who work for him during the harvests. But I don't think they harvest anything. They don't come in work clothes."

Gonzalo looked up from the notepad he was scribbling into.

"You say, you saw these men a month or two ago?"

"Yes, a month or two ago."

"You have been a tremendous help, Don Julio. Not everyone can remember a person they saw a month or two ago."

"It's not that hard. I saw them today again, too."

"Today?"

"Today. The same men, the same Jeep. The wind brought the smoke right into my house; I went out to the road to see what was happening, and there they were, driving past the house. Maybe they came from the road on the other side of the property."

"Are you sure it was the same men, Don Julio?"

"Of course. One of them waved to me." Don Julio crossed his arms again, a sign that he was a little miffed at not being believed.

"Which way were they headed, Don Julio?"

"Well, first they went toward Comerio, you know, toward the clinic. Later, they came back toward the town."

Don Julio was gesturing to show Gonzalo the general directions the car had traveled in as though the sheriff didn't know his own town, but Gonzalo had turned back toward his squad car already. He drove away a minute later. Don Julio went back to his guests who had not been able to pick up enough of the conversation to quench their thirst for gossip.

"What did the sheriff want?" somebody asked.

"Like always. Asking questions. He wanted me to solve the whole case for him," was Don Julio's reply and he went inside to satisfy his guests' curiosity.

CHAPTER SIX

The fire engine was driven calmly into the valley that separated the plaza from the Ortiz house because, as the former mayor said, "The house was made of wood and is probably smoldering on the ground already." Ramirez asked to be dropped off at a point only some thousand yards short of the fire, giving the driver the simple direction that he should continue straight on the road he was already on. From the point Ramirez dismounted, however, the smoke of the extinguished fire was no longer visible. The driver somehow got off the road he was on without noticing it and drove on until he saw a sign in which the town of Angustias bid farewell. Then he drove the truck into a driveway to make a U-turn, only to find that the driveway was too narrow to serve that purpose. He backed up most of the way to the point where he had left Ramirez, one of his uniformed brothers walking before the retreating truck to watch for oncoming

8

traffic that might otherwise speed around a bend in the mountain road with disastrous results. At this point, the driver started again in his search for the smoking building and finally found it. Calderon and Collazo were standing out in front as the crew dismounted.

"You guys called about a fire?" the crew chief asked. He was slowly putting on his gear, knowing that it wouldn't be needed.

"We put it out," Calderon answered. "It's a crime scene, so we can't have you guys in there right now."

"Is the fire suspicious?" the chief asked.

"Nope. They left the gasoline can inside. It was arson without a doubt."

"Can I take a look through the window?" the chief asked.

It was clear to Calderon that he wanted to feel useful, so she waved him on. He sloshed through water that had pooled in front of the house from what was draining through the flooring. The house was dark inside as most of the Miami windows had been rolled shut and Calderon had closed the door. She used her flashlight to illuminate the smoky inside.

"That might be where they started the fire," Calderon said, shining her light on the splayed legs of Pedro Ortiz. "They also splashed some gasoline on a little girl," she said, highlighting the corner where Pedro's daughter had lain. "The mother was burned also, but not so badly. I can show you her body from the window on the side if you want."

"No, no," the firefighter replied. "I think I've seen enough."

"Well, the rest of the gasoline I think was spilled in the center of the floor in the front room here," Calderon continued, but the fire chief was already walking back toward his truck, using a handkerchief to mop his brow and upper lip.

"Just remember to look for clues under the house," he yelled to her from inside his truck.

"Under? Why?"

"If the water flowed there, it might have carried something worth knowing about, no? Anyway, be sure to call us if you need us."

The truck pulled away and drove off, leaving Collazo and Calderon on the lawn.

"Do you want me to check under the house?" Collazo asked.

"No. I figure anything under there has no place to go really. It'll be there whenever the area dries out."

"That could be days, *mi'ja*."

Calderon thought for a moment. In the end, she knew it was not right to ask Collazo to do the dirty work of the department. There was also the consideration that Collazo's further involvement might be used as a sign that the evidence was contaminated or that the officers of Angustias were incapable of doing their jobs.

Calderon sat on a large rock near where the Ortiz property let out to the road, and she invited Collazo to join her.

"You're not going to grow any taller by standing like that," she coaxed him, but he had a restless look on his face.

"I should really either do something or go home," he answered.

"Well, keep me company; that's something. Gonzalo might want you to relieve me of watching this site; when he comes from talking to Don Julio, I'll flag him down, and we can see if he needs you out here anymore today."

A minute passed by the two in silence, and then Gonzalo's squad car pulled out of Don Julio's driveway. Officer Calderon jumped up and waved an arm-length wave, but Gonzalo was intent on driving and headed straight for town without so much as looking her way. She pulled the walkie-talkie from her gun belt only to find that the heat of the fire had wilted the antenna and made the unit useless, first sputtering to life for a moment, then just dying away into a quiet electric hum.

"I'm going to search the property and see if I can figure out any more of this mess," Collazo told her.

"Don't go near the crime scene," Calderon reminded him, and he walked off into the woods.

Hector had sped after the two men in the Jeep with the intention of making sure they had nothing to do with the murders of that morning. How to achieve this goal was not clear to him, however, and he could make no headway in the matter while driving to town. After all, there was no probable cause for him to stop them or to speak with them. He hoped that he could catch up to them and then observe them either commit some infraction or appear lost. They certainly weren't from town, nor were they visitors he had ever noticed before. In a town as small as Angustias, they stood out.

He did not catch up to the Jeep. He drove straight into town without catching a glimpse of them at all. The thought flashed through his mind that the Jeep driver might have pulled off into one of the many driveways and stayed hidden among the overgrown weeds that prevailed almost everywhere along the road. Or perhaps they had pulled away into one of the side roads that led to other towns in the center of the island. As he parked in front of the station house, he nodded to himself, enjoying the comforting thought that the men might simply have been lost earlier and finally found their way out of Angustias and he would not have to think about confronting them at all.

"They probably had nothing to do with it," he said out loud to himself as he opened the precinct door.

"You guys got big problems?" the prisoner in the cell at the back yelled out to him as he entered.

"Go back to sleep, Carlos," Hector told him.

"No, man. I want to know what happened. I heard there was a fire."

Carlos was sitting on the edge of his cot. He had taken off his shirt and sneakers and was rubbing the thighs of his dirty trousers as though trying to bring warmth into them. He stopped to scratch lazily at his bony chest.

"Come on, I have a right to know."

Hector ignored him. He was busy working with his collected evidence. He placed the prints he had lifted from the Ortiz truck with clear tape onto a white paper background and sent them by fax to San Juan with a note explaining the urgent nature of his request for processing. There they had computer databases where they would compare the prints to those of people who had been through the criminal justice system. It was a slow process, but the Ortiz case was likely to be the only double homicide on the island, so there would be an answer back within a couple of hours, a day at most. So, at least, Hector hoped.

"I need to go to the bathroom," Carlos continued from his cell.

"So go. There's a toilet right next to your cot."

"Where's the paper?"

A quick look showed Hector that the prisoner had a point. He fished out a fresh roll of toilet paper from a supply cabinet and stuffed it through the bars of the cell. Carlos took it and sat on his cot again.

"I thought you had to go," Hector said.

"I'll wait till you're gone. Come on, tell me what's going on?"

"I'm very busy right now, Carlos. If you wanted to be treated like every other citizen, you shouldn't have attacked a police officer."

"I did that?"

"You hit Officer Calderon. You punched her in the gut. You're lucky she didn't kill you."

"You screwing her?"

The comment made Hector look up from the evidence vouchers he was filling out. He got the spare cell key out of Gonzalo's desk drawer and strode calmly but purposefully to the cell door. He opened up and entered the small room. Carlos could see the quiet anger seething in the deputy and shrunk back in his cot. He put his hands out in front of him. Hector leaned in close but didn't touch the prisoner.

"If you talk like that again, I will hurt you. Do you understand me, Carlos? I will put my badge and my gun away and I will fight you like a man. You like punching women? Well, let me tell you, if you talk about, look at, or even think about Officer Calderon again, I will break you into pieces and they won't know how to put you back together again. In fact, I can't think of anyone who would bother to try. Are you thinking about Officer Calderon right now?"

"Officer who?" Carlos answered from his cringe. Somewhere in the back of his mind he was hoping this answer would please Hector, but if it did, Hector didn't show it.

"I need to work on those papers for two more minutes. Then I'm going to get you some lunch. Don't say another word to me today, okay?"

Carlos nodded and locked his lips in pantomime. Hector locked down the cell and returned the key to its place. He finished his work in silence and went out.

Prisoner lunches are simple affairs: generally just a sandwich and a coffee. Three or four different places were used by the sheriff's office. The fact that there wasn't a single place that all prisoners were fed from was no indication that prisoners were catered to at all. Instead it highlighted the simple fact that the different police officers had different tastes and the prisoner lunchtime was also lunchtime for the officers. Hector's favorite place was across the plaza adjacent to the Roman Catholic church. They served sloppy hamburgers there with any topping you could want and crinkled French fries lightly peppered. When Hector left the station house, he was in search of one of these hamburgers for himself and a ham and cheese sandwich for Carlos. What he found as soon as he made his way onto the plaza and glanced toward the church was the black Jeep.

The car was empty and parked directly in front of the church. Hector took a quick look around the plaza, hoping to find either driver or passenger. Not seeing them, he got out his radio and tried raising Gonzalo, without luck. He undid the snap holding his pistol in place and walked quickly across the plaza toward the church. He turned off his radio before going in.

It was as Hector entered the cool air and muted lights of the church that Gonzalo drove out of Don Julio's driveway and got onto his radio trying to contact Hector. He wanted to warn his deputy about the possible threat the Jeep riders posed. "Hector, Hector, respond," the sheriff called, but Hector, radio off, dipped his fingers into a small bowl holding holy water that was recessed into one of the columns and crossed himself before starting his search.

CHAPTER SEVEN

With Rafael Ramirez taking a ride home with the fire truck, Jorge Nuñez, the former deputy mayor of Angustias, had nothing to do on the plaza. He sat. He thought about the events of the day so far and wondered if there was a way he could help. Jorge was one of those rare politicians who did not want anything out of political life but to help his fellow citizens. Did he enjoy the honor and respect that had been accorded him in return for his services? Certainly. He would not have been human if they made no impact on his psyche. But he would have worked as hard and cared as much without these rewards. In fact, he had always worked at the side of Rafael Ramirez, who was naturally brash and abrasive and had often found a way to leave a mess behind himself that needed cleaning up if headway were to be made against the city's problems. The moments were rare when Jorge Nuñez was in the spotlight. His work usually began after the mayor had done something to absorb the attention of the entire town.

In the heat of the sun, Jorge could think of nothing he could do that would be useful. He rose from his bench and straightened out his *guayabera* shirt, took off his Panama hat, and ran fingers through his hair before readjusting it on his head. He took a long look at his watch and decided to visit the current mayor. There might be some small service a retired official might be able to render or perhaps a word of advice wanted.

The inside of the city government building, the *alcaldia,* was cool. The floors were tiled in ceramic as were the fronts of each step leading into the building. There was a pay phone in the lobby as well as a water fountain and a long padded bench running against one wall—amenities that had not been thought necessary when Ramirez and Nuñez had been in office. They had prided themselves in never having anyone wait to see them if they had a problem. People did wait, of course, but never for very long, and never without being told how long it would be before they could be seen. The lobby was otherwise empty that day, and Nuñez walked through to the mayor's office. Like Ramirez before him, he also noted the changes in décor. Unlike Ramirez, he appreciated them.

Francisco Primavera and the deputy mayor, Miguel Belen, were at the mayor's desk. Primavera was on the phone, sitting and listening while Miguel Belen was standing with the palms of his hands flat on the desktop. Sunlight streamed through the open windows, and shadows gave Primavera's face something of an ominous aspect. He was clearly agitated and waiting his turn to speak.

"This is just one big mess down here. He's running around like a chicken without a head," Jorge Nuñez heard. "You better do something soon. Hold on a minute." Primavera placed his palm over the receiver and looked at Nuñez. Miguel Belen looked at the man he had succeeded from his position at the desk.

"Do you or Ramirez ever knock?" Primavera asked. "How can I help you?"

"Who is running around like a chicken?" Nuñez asked.

"What?"

"I said who is running around like a chicken?"

"Oh," Primavera took his hand off the receiver and asked the person on the other end if he could call back in two minutes.

"Look, Nuñez, I don't want to be rude, but there is a little emergency, and I am trying to handle it as best as I can, okay?"

"Sure."

"I'm sure you realize that Sheriff Gonzalo is in over his head here. He needs help, and I'm trying to get him some. You understand, don't you?"

"Gonzalo's a very capable investigator—"

Primavera cut off Nuñez with a deep sigh. Miguel Belen stood up straight, walked over to a leather chair, and took a seat.

"I'm sure Gonzalo can handle a lot of things, but this is getting a little out of control. Trust me on this; I have more information about the situation than you do."

The mayor started to dial a number on his phone. He put the receiver to his ear, listening for the rings. He looked up with a bit of surprise to see that Nuñez hadn't shown himself out.

"Can I help you at all?" he asked.

"That's what I'm here to ask you," Nuñez answered. Apparently whomever Primavera was calling picked up the phone.

"Yeah, can you hold just a minute?" Primavera said into the phone. He looked up at Nuñez again.

"Look, if you want to help, find Gonzalo and tell him not to touch evidence if he doesn't absolutely have to. We're going to have professionals here as soon as I can get them, okay? Oh, and make sure the door actually closes as you go out, thank you." Primavera turned back to his phone call, and Nuñez saw himself out.

In the lobby, a young man sprang up from the padded bench and offered Nuñez his hand. He had a big smile on his face and he wore shades though the lobby was not brightly lit. The young man wore baggy shorts that reached past his knees and a completely unbuttoned shirt with a white undershirt. Nuñez took the hand that was offered him.

"Are you the mayor?" the young man asked.

"No. The mayor's in his office." Nuñez thumbed toward the firmly shut door. "I don't think he wants to see anyone."

"Oh," the young man said. "I'll wait."

He sat down again, still smiling, and Nuñez walked out into the sunlight.

Making sure the two men he sought were not in the nave of the church took Hector only a minute or so. Among all the pews there was only one person, Doña Fidela. Fidela was a squat woman, barely visible as she sat near the front of the church praying the rosary. She was only sixty years of age but had been a widow for more than twenty years; she had exchanged her grief for piety, but a second grief was coming to her slowly: she was going blind and wore thick glasses that were of questionable value to her. Hector approached her quietly.

"Doña Fidela," he whispered. She ignored him.

"Doña Fidela, this is very important. Have any men been in here? Maybe in the last five minutes?"

"I'm praying," she whispered back.

"I understand that, but I'm looking for some men who might be very dangerous. Has anyone been in here?"

Doña Fidela stopped moving her hands along the beads of the rosary and thought a moment before responding.

"I haven't seen anyone, *mi'jo*. My eyes are not so good anymore."

"Oh, I know, but maybe you heard something."

"My son, I don't hear so well anymore, either. I don't think any-one came in here in the last half-hour, but if they were quiet, I wouldn't know about it. I can't help you. Maybe you can try talking with the young priest. I know he went to the offices in the back a little while ago."

Hector genuflected before the altar and made his way to a series of small offices toward the back of the church. The young priest Doña Fidela had mentioned was Father Moreno, newly graduated from seminary and one of two priests at the parish.

"How can I help you, Hector?"

Hector had met the new priest on a handful of occasions with-out growing to like him. The man seemed to look down upon everyone he came across as though he really were more holy than they. Perhaps most annoying was that in every other respect he did seem holier than most.

"I'm looking for two men who may have come into the church, Father. They were driving a black Jeep that's parked out in front—"

"Yes, yes. I know who you're talking about, but they didn't enter the church. Of course, if they had, you know they would be able to ask for sanctuary—"

It was Hector's turn to interrupt. "Of course, and Father Diego over in Naranjito would be the one to decide on whether the church wanted to extend that courtesy. Did you happen to see where the men went?"

"Yes, I did. Are these men wanted for anything in particular, Hector?"

"It's a police matter, Father. Could you please tell me where they went?"

"Certainly, certainly. They went into the *alcaldia*. I was crossing the plaza coming toward the church when they got out of their car. One of them waved to me, in fact. They seemed very nice."

"Not everything is as it seems," Hector threw over his shoulder as he left the office and the church.

At the same time that Hector was having his conversations with Doña Fidela and Father Moreno inside the church, Gonzalo was parking in front of the station house. He hadn't really had a moment to think through the case; he would have liked some peace, even if it were only for a few minutes so that he could better piece together the events of the day and all the information he had learned about a citizen he had sworn to protect but had apparently not at all known. When *Los Metropolitanos* came riding into town, he usually liked to have all the details of a case in their proper places; he hated the idea of giving someone else credit for work he knew he was able to do himself if given the chance.

He was also disturbed by the news about the Jeep and its occupants, but he didn't want to jump the gun. He told himself how unwise it would be to pour any of his limited resources into chasing someone who may have no connection at all to the case. Still, while Don Julio may not have been the most reliable witness possible, he was not prone to simply making up stories. And if those men had anything to do with the murders, then they were to be considered armed and dangerous—not exactly people he wanted to leave unattended in Angustias.

From his cell, Carlos derailed Gonzalo's train of thought before it had gotten a chance to get going. "Where's my food, Gonzalo? I'm dying of hunger here."

"Hector will get you something to eat as soon as he comes in, now just stay quiet, okay?"

"Hector? He came and went already. He said he was going to get me a sandwich about an hour ago, and he never came back."

"That's impossible. Hector was ahead of me by no more than ten minutes. Go back to sleep, Carlos, and I'll get you a sandwich myself, okay?"

"I don't know. Maybe you should just give me the keys. I'll get my own sandwich and lock myself up again. It could be like that show that used to come on with Andy Griffith. You remember that?"

Gonzalo was about to tell Carlos to shut up; he was about to walk out of his office since there was no chance for a peaceful moment of reflection there. He opened his mouth and closed it again, realizing the futility of any further words with Carlos. He turned toward the door and in that instant a shot rang out on the plaza of Angustias. Gonzalo froze in his tracks for a moment, not sure of what he had heard. There was more gunfire and a screeching of car tires.

"Go, Gonzalo!" Carlos called to him, and he went.

Gonzalo ran out to the street and turned the corner toward the plaza. His gun was drawn and what he saw startled him, presenting him with a situation he didn't immediately know how to handle though the scene seemed to unfold in slow motion.

The black Jeep was speeding on the pavement of the plaza in serious jeopardy of running over a mother leading her toddler by the hand. Hector was running at full speed behind the Jeep. The mother jerked her child up into her arms and dodged away from the car and out of its path. The driver shot another two rounds over his shoulder but came nowhere near to hitting Hector, who kept running.

At this point the driver of the Jeep swerved off the plaza in order to avoid running into a cement bench. Hector cut his path to intercept the Jeep; Gonzalo could see now that Hector's weapon was in hand. Hector took a running step onto another of the plaza's benches and leaped into the air on a trajectory that would put him within reach of the Jeep driver. The driver, a young light-skinned man, took another shot at the deputy, firing across his own body, wildly. Gonzalo's heart skipped several beats as he watched Hector fall out of his flight, flipping in the air before hitting the curb of the plaza, landing on the back of his neck, flopping onto his stomach, and skidding a foot or two before coming to a perfect rest on the ground.

Gonzalo raised his pistol in both hands and kept his aim on the driver. He shouted for him to stop and get out of the car, but the driver most likely didn't hear him, and was not likely to have paid him any attention anyway. The Jeep pulled up short in front of the *alcaldia,* and Gonzalo was ready to take his shot. He knew he had the young man's head in plain view and he was standing only a dozen yards away. It was a shot he could safely take, but just then a door opened behind the Jeep, and one of the residents of the houses lining the plaza came out to see what was happening.

The young lady stood maybe twenty yards behind the Jeep. Gonzalo yelled for her to get down. The driver of the Jeep found the sheriff and fired off two rounds from a semiautomatic weapon in Gonzalo's general direction. The sheriff of Angustias stood his ground, using one hand to motion the young lady to get back inside, but she stood there, not frozen in fear but instead confused as to why he was signaling her. She had apparently not associated the sounds with a shoot-out.

Another young man came running down the stairs of the city's official building and hopped into the back of the Jeep. The driver shot at Gonzalo again; he hit an edge of the building. A piece of cement chipped off and hit Gonzalo above his right eye. Gonzalo ducked then, using the hand he had been waving with to clutch at his eye and bringing his gun-hand down to his side. He lost his footing and stumbled into a bank of hostas at the side of the *alcaldia* as the Jeep sped by him. When he looked up, the man who sat at the back of the Jeep was waving at him and smiling.

CHAPTER EIGHT

For those not accustomed to thinking of land in terms of acreage, it is difficult to imagine an acre. Ten acres are equal to a fair-sized shopping mall. The land Pedro Ortiz owned and worked comprised thirty-seven acres that were mostly wooded with fruit trees. Pedro had always kept one small field of about three acres clear of trees; the area was watered by a small stream and here he planted *gandules*, pigeon peas, and locally popular tubers like *malanga* and *yautia*. This field was not far from his house. Farther from the Ortiz home there was another treeless field where he let his animals graze—a dozen or so goats and a half-dozen sheep, all destined for the butcher near Christmastime, and a cow with calf that supplied the family with milk and butter. Near there Pedro had also built a pen for two or three hogs that he would slaughter himself around Christmas and Three Kings Day.

Collazo went to see the animals first. The chickens ranged freely and would survive on bugs. The hogs would need to be fed, but the other livestock had enough grass and water themselves. Collazo had only recently given up tending livestock himself and felt a curiosity to see how the younger farmer had been keeping up with the demands of the work. He cast his eye on the cow and calf first. The mother looked at him as she chewed her cud as though she knew him, and he was happy to oblige her with a few stalks of a tall grass he knew she would like. Both animals were in fine health, but there was a large tick attached to the mother's rear leg only a little above and behind the hoof, an impossible place for the cow to scratch. Collazo made a note to himself to remove it later.

There was a lot of money in raising goats and sheep for slaughter, but Collazo had never appreciated the animals themselves. He liked cows and loathed goats; cows had an intelligent look in their eyes while the face of a goat always seemed to imply sheathed deception: they had too often gotten away from him and eaten his crops with the voracity they used in eating anything else they got hold of for him to be able to love them much. Sheep were not much better and had the added detraction of being woolly—it did not take much for the wool to begin to look like mange. Unless one raised sheep in large numbers, a situation that sounded like hell to Collazo, their wool was just a nuisance. For Collazo, both types of animals shared the saving grace that they tasted good and so it was a pleasure to kill them. These animals paid him no mind as he walked past them on his way to the hogs.

The stench from the area was powerful and there were only three animals. Collazo wondered what it would have smelled like if there were a dozen. They came up to the fence when they saw him. He couldn't imagine what it must be like for the *Americanos* who actually kept their pigs inside a barn all day feeding them at one end and collecting their waste from the other. How could anyone get in the building with the pigs? he thought to himself.

There was a little shack next to the hogs' pen. The door was unlocked. Inside was a burlap sack containing fruit skins, some grains, and rotting vegetables. There were also chicken bones and two rats sitting on the top of the sack eating. Each rat was at least six inches long, not counting the tails. Collazo was sure there were roaches as well, but the rats were more important. Both watched him, but neither moved as he approached the sack. He closed the sack with them inside, and their squirming came too late to do them any good. He carried the sack, which weighed forty pounds or more, and dumped it over the wood fence that kept the hogs. The three animals bit through the cloth to get at their food. The hog at the top end found a rat beneath the burlap with his first bite and brought the rodent up through the tear he made. The other rat tried to flee through that same hole but was caught by the tail.

Hogs are bad business, Collazo thought. One had bitten him early in his farming career and that had ended his attempt to raise any others. He made another mental note to suggest transporting the animals to a butcher soon since there were no other sacks of food in the shack, and he wasn't about to start caring for them at his age.

This mental note brought Collazo to something of a conundrum. How would the animals be transported? The sty wasn't too far from the house and the road, but the most direct path was wooded and steep. Other paths might be easier, but longer. Hogs were not that easy to herd. Come to think of it, how would Pedro have gotten any of the animals to the field they inhabited? They couldn't have been brought in from the side of the property the house was on; you don't just herd goats through woods. He looked around.

There was a path on the far side of the open field. It was broad enough to admit a car or truck, and Collazo decided to investigate it. Not only would he need to know if the animals could be gotten out that way, but he also suspected that the path might have been how the killers got onto the property and off it again without calling too much attention to themselves.

The path curved and led near to the spot where the cocaine had been burned and a shot had been put in Pedro Ortiz's leg. Collazo stayed off the path itself, walking in the woods parallel to it. He could see tire marks in the orange dust of the road. He followed on this course until he reached a fence made of two strands of barbed wire strung along tree trunks and cut branches that had been stabbed into the ground. The fence was down where the path was. He put the strands back onto the nails that normally held them to an orange tree slowly being choked by vines.

Though it had changed much since he had last worked there as a day laborer in the 1930s, Collazo could still recognize the land the path crossed into. There were trees now where once there had only been a slightly inclined field of tobacco, but the land had belonged to Martin Alonso Mendoza, and now it belonged to that man's grandson of the same name. From where he stood, Collazo could tell that the road trampled through tall grass for another two hundred yards before letting out onto the same road that passed in front of the Ortiz house after a twist or two. From this same position, he could see the same black Jeep Hector had been worried about pull up to a halt by the fence that kept Mendoza's property from the road. The driver got out and pulled away a few dead branches that hid the entrance from passing cars. He drove the car through and dismounted again to replace the branches. By the time he got into the Jeep the second time, Collazo had already made good progress in racing back toward the Ortiz home and Iris Calderon.

Gonzalo had lifted himself out of the bed of hosta plants and had raised his gun in the direction of the Jeep, but the passenger in the back was no longer looking his way and the car turned a corner and left his sight. Gonzalo got on his radio as he rushed to Hector's side, but he could raise none of his deputies. This was not unusual in the mountains and valleys of Angustias, and Gonzalo thought nothing of it. Hector was his one concern. He repeated to himself a thought that had entered his mind on idle occasions: Hector can't be killed. The deputy had proven indestructible over the years. He had been shot at more than once, someone had slashed at him with a machete, and he had been in a car wreck and a motorcycle wreck. In fact, it was a joke between Gonzalo and Mari that Hector led a charmed life except in love. Still, the short run to Hector's side seemed unendurably long.

Gonzalo holstered his gun and knelt beside his deputy. Hector's eyes were closed, but his right hand was trembling palm-down on the pavement.

"Where are you hit?" Gonzalo asked, taking the young man's hand.

"My vest took it. The bullet hit at an angle, but I think I broke a rib when I came down," Hector answered calmly. He tried to raise himself, his eyes still closed, but he didn't even get his head off the ground.

"Stay down a minute. Let me help you turn over."

Gonzalo helped Hector to sit up, using his leg as a prop. He opened Hector's shirt and undid the Velcro that fastened together his bulletproof vest. A Kevlar vest will certainly stop a bullet, but it doesn't do the job painlessly. A shot from close range will feel like a blow with a baseball bat, which is not something one would want to go through twice. This shot had glanced off the deputy's chest, so it wasn't nearly the full impact Hector could have expected at close range, but his fall had been uncontrolled. Later, Hector would find that he had a hairline fracture in one of his ribs. More importantly, he suffered a throbbing headache from his fall. He felt dizzy when he tried to stand up, and Gonzalo coached him to rest on one knee for a while before attempting to stand up straight again. Hector did as he was told, closed his eyes, and took several deep breaths.

"Do you think you need to go to the clinic right now?" Gonzalo asked.

It was reasonable to take Hector for medical examination; in fact, it was a departmental regulation. But then, Angustias had cold-blooded killers on the loose, and Gonzalo needed every officer out in the field.

"Do you think those guys are going to come back?" Hector asked.

"They're sticking around for something. They're looking for something. I think they'll keep coming back until they get what they're looking for."

"All right then, I'll get back to work."

Hector stood up and stretched gingerly, then grinned at his sheriff. There were scratches on his face and a small knot forming over his left eye.

"Don't worry about me, boss. I'll go check on Calderon and Collazo. First, I'll get Carlos a sandwich."

"Don't forget to check in with San Juan about the prints," Gonzalo answered. "And take some aspirin."

"Got it. Where are you going to be?"

"I'll be out in the field soon enough. I still have a couple homes I'd like to visit to see if I can get any more information on these two characters; maybe they have friends in the area I should know about. I've got to see the mayor first, though."

Hector dusted himself off and walked toward the same burger shop he had started out for what seemed like ages earlier.

"Hey, Hector. Turn your radio back on, okay?"

Hector gave him the·thumbs-up sign without turning around. He fiddled with the radio on his gun belt.

It dawned on Gonzalo then that he hadn't really communicated with his deputies about this case so far except for a minimal transfer of information and the orders he gave. He made a note to get them all together at the Ortiz house and have them share everything they had learned about the case. He would meet up with Calderon there in a few minutes. Before that he would have to speak with the mayor. The mayor could put out the information about the two men in the Jeep.

Gonzalo looked up at the *alcaldia*. The double doors were ajar slightly, and as he walked toward them, they opened more fully and the mayor put his head out slowly, looked around, and then stepped outside. Gonzalo took the steps to the door two by two and stopped in front of the mayor.

"We need to talk," Gonzalo said.

"I agree," said the mayor, and he led the way into the building and toward his office.

A few hundred yards from the Ortiz home, Officers Jimenez and Ramos were questioning another Ortiz neighbor. The conversations they had had up to that point with the people of the area had been less than illuminating. One teenage girl had made up an elaborate tale about having seen a group of men fleeing the scene right before the first officers had arrived to put out the fire. The officers asked about and recorded into their notepads detailed descriptions of each of the men in the group, but their interest weakened when they figured out that all the men looked alike except they looked different. Their interest died out completely when they found that the men had driven off in a limousine.

"If anyone had come through Angustias in a limousine, they

would have been seen, don't you think?" Officer Ramos asked the girl. She shrugged in reply, and the officers closed their pads and left.

Both men had also come up against several people who refused to give any information. It was widely understood that the Ortiz family had been murdered, and several neighbors told the officers quite plainly that they had no intention of standing as witnesses against murderers who might come back at any moment.

"With all the respect you deserve," one housewife told them, "you guys are *gandules*. If I give you information, and these people come back, you guys can't do anything to protect me."

"We're police officers, we carry guns," Officer Jimenez said.

The woman stooped to take a close look at the gun he carried in his gun belt; Jimenez stood still for the inspection. She straightened and crossed her arms.

"I gave one like that to my nephew for Christmas," she said.

Jimenez and Ramos spent the next five minutes convincing her to tell all she knew. When she finally cracked, it turned out she had nothing to say that would have been of any use. The Ortizes were regular in all the company they kept, in the hours they worked, the arguments they had over issues large and small. There was no unusual activity to report except, of course, for the fire that morning. No unusual sounds had been heard except, of course, for some loud salsa music for a few minutes before the fire; probably some teenagers in a car passing through. This was all that Ramos and Jimenez had been able to gather from the lady, and it was all they were able to gather from the other houses they canvassed. They drew nearer to the Ortiz farm.

The Ortiz home was visible from the entrance to the property of Don Ernesto Figueroa, but vegetation blocked the view after only a step or two. Though Don Figueroa was more than seventy years old, he kept the grass in his yard neatly trimmed with a machete that he kept at razor sharpness; to a farmer in the lushness of the tropics, a dull machete blade represents a waste of time and energy. Why strike a weed twice when once could have sufficed?

Officer Ramos noticed the contrast of the neatness of Don Figueroa's yard and the overgrowth of the property that stretched between that and Pedro Ortiz's farm.

"Who owns that land?" he asked as soon as Don Figueroa opened his door.

"Martin Mendoza," Don Figueroa replied without having to think twice. His tone indicated that he couldn't imagine anyone not knowing the extent of Mendoza's property.

Ramos took another look into the dense underbrush.

"And where does this Mendoza live, do you know?" Ramos asked.

Don Figueroa readjusted his glasses and pinched the tip of his nose between thumb and forefinger a couple of times in quick succession. He glanced from Ramos to Jimenez and back again. It was clear from all this that he felt he was contemplating an ignorance so profound that he didn't know where to begin explaining.

"Martin Mendoza is the richest man in Angustias. He's one of the richest men on the whole island. He's a millionaire. He was born that way. I used to work for his grandfather. I worked for his father, and I used to work for him." Don Figueroa looked down his nose and over his glasses at the officers still standing at his doorway.

"But where does he live?" Ramos pressed.

"Wherever he wants," Don Figueroa answered. He held his hands in front of him palms up, as though to indicate that there was no more he could do for the officers if they weren't going to put any effort into thinking the problem out.

Officer Ramos jotted Martin Mendoza's name into his notepad and decided to drop that line of inquiry. He could ask Gonzalo later about this millionaire. He moved on to the basic set of questions about suspicious people and noises that he had asked several others previously. There had not been anything out of the ordinary at the Ortiz property in the past few days or weeks. The officers thanked Don Figueroa and turned back toward their car.

"What you really should do is talk to Martin Mendoza," Don Figueroa said.

"What for?" Ramos asked. He was willing to investigate any possibility that might break the monotonous string of pointless interrogations.

"These guys have been driving onto his property every few days—guys in a Jeep. They were there this morning."

"How could they drive through that forest even in a Jeep?"

"Through the other side." Don Figueroa walked through his small wooden house toward a back door and the officers followed him.

Part of Martin Mendoza's field was visible from Don Figueroa's back door. What could be seen was much less overrun by wild vegetation than the part that could be seen from the front door, and there was a definite path leading off the main road. A grove of trees and the start of heavy foliage hid more than this from view. Don Figueroa pointed out the extent of the Mendoza property in that area, showing how it ballooned out behind both the Ortiz land and his own and how it dipped into the valley and climbed most of the way up a distant hill.

Officer Ramos asked some questions about the men and the Jeep and when these trespassings had begun, and Don Figueroa was a fountain of information.

"I don't know why these men show up, but they aren't farming the land. They might be squatters you know. People do that some-times. The courts can give them the land if they prove that they lived there long enough. That's why I say you should talk to Martin Mendoza. He might get himself into legal trouble. Imagine if one of these guys breaks his leg on the property. They might sue him even though they are the ones trespassing. That's how people are nowadays. Brazen."

Ramos scribbled another note or two into his pad.

"In fact, there they go now." Don Figueroa pointed at the path in Mendoza's field where the Jeep with two riders was making its way.

Ramos and Jimenez strained to get a good look, but they were far too distant to make out any facial features or a license plate number. Ramos closed his notepad and buttoned it into his left shirt pocket. He thanked Don Figueroa for his help and he and Jimenez walked back to the squad car.

"Should we confront them?" Jimenez asked.

"I think it would be a waste to spend our time talking to those guys. Officer Calderon is in the Ortiz house. We'll tell her about this. It's probably nothing."

CHAPTER NINE

As soon as the door of the *alcaldia* closed behind him, Gonzalo fired a question at the mayor's back. "What did that guy want here?"

Francisco Primavera kept walking toward his office. He held up a hand without looking back, signaling Gonzalo either to be silent or to be patient, the sheriff could not tell which.

The office door opened slowly before the mayor got to it. Gonzalo knew that the unseen hand was that of Miguel Belen, the new deputy mayor. He tried, in that instant, to figure out where Belen had come from. He wasn't originally from Angustias, that much Gonzalo knew, but he couldn't decide in the few steps into the office how long ago the deputy mayor had moved into town, and he couldn't decide if the train of thought had any value at that moment.

As soon as they were in the office and Belen had shut the door, Primavera had a question of his own.

"Why didn't you shoot that guy?"

"How about you answer my question first?" Gonzalo shot back.

"Okay, how about we try this a different way? Let's pretend that I am the mayor and you are the sheriff. I ask the questions and you answer them. How does that sound?"

"I don't think I like this game, Primavera. I need answers here . . ."

"Hold on, sheriff." Primavera took a step closer to Gonzalo and jabbed a finger in his face. "I plan on remaining the mayor. If you don't like this game, then you can just stop being the sheriff. So far I can't think of anyone who would do a worse job . . ."

" 'A worse job'? What are you talking about?"

"We have a whole family that was murdered. The killers drove right into town, they walked into City Hall, they shot at one of your deputies, they shot at you, and you let them get right past you without even firing a shot. Did Officer Pareda even shoot at the guy that was driving?"

"No."

"And why is that?"

"I was in his line of fire."

"I thought he was supposed to a be a perfect shot."

"He's the best shot anywhere on this island. An unsafe shot is still unsafe no matter how good you are. That's the definition of unsafe."

"Okay. Fine. Why didn't you shoot the guy yourself?"

"One of your fine citizens came out of her house. She was in my line of fire. It was an unsafe shot."

"Are you just making this up?"

Gonzalo threw his hands up in disgust. The mayor had chosen precisely the wrong moment to question his integrity. He turned to leave the office. No one moved to stop him. The sheriff stopped himself.

"You never answered my question."

Primavera walked around his desk and took a seat.

"What question, Sheriff?"

"What did that guy want in here?"

"He said he was looking for money."

"He asked you for money?"

"No, Gonzalo. He didn't ask me for it. He told me he was looking for a bag full of money. That's why he's still around. He said Pedro Ortiz had stolen a million dollars from him, and that he wasn't going to leave this town alone until he got the money back."

"Was that all he said?"

"He was only in here for a minute before the shooting started, and then he ran out."

"Did he say anything else? Anything at all?"

"Nothing."

"Did he have any kind of accent? Was he from the city or the countryside? Was he from New York, maybe?"

"I didn't notice. He spoke Spanish like I do, so I don't think he was from New York. Do people from the city have a different accent?"

"They speak a little faster sometimes."

Gonzalo turned again to go. He saw Miguel Belen sitting in an armchair next to the door. He had on sunglasses and his arms were crossed.

Gonzalo stopped with his hand on the doorknob.

"Where are you from?" he asked the deputy mayor.

"Ponce" was the answer.

"Did you hear the young man ask or say anything that the mayor may have forgotten?"

Deputy Mayor Belen shrugged.

"I'm going to sign out a shotgun to you," Gonzalo told Belen, and then he left the office.

He was back a few minutes later and handed the shotgun to the deputy mayor.

"If the bastard comes back, do me a favor and put a hole in him, okay?"

"Not a problem," Belen answered.

"Oh, and by the way. Not that it means much." Gonzalo was speaking now to the mayor. "But you'll be happy to know that the whole Ortiz family wasn't murdered. The children survived."

A look passed between Primavera and Belen and the mayor said, "Well, thank God for small miracles." Gonzalo left the office wishing he knew what was behind the mayor's declaration.

Once back out on the street, Gonzalo made a beeline for the only bank in town, a small institution on one of the streets leading away from the plaza. Only two years earlier, Gonzalo and his deputies had fought a desperate gun battle against thugs with automatic weapons and bulletproof vests. Several of his officers had been hit on the sidewalk in front of the bank, one of them had been killed, and the blood of the officers had mingled with the blood of innocent victims and of the criminals and trickled down the street along the gutter that day. In the time since the investigation had been closed on that case, Gonzalo had rarely been back to the bank, preferring to let Mari do the banking when it was needed.

He stopped a moment at the spot where he had checked Officer Almodovar for a pulse and found she didn't have one. Though he felt slightly silly, he squatted on the spot and put his fingers to the sidewalk where her blood had been. The memory of the moment came back to him vividly, and his hand started to tremble. He stood up to avoid embarrassing himself.

The emotions brought out by the inside of the bank were no less powerful. Within a few steps of the door, Gonzalo glanced down at the spot where the eighteen-year-old security guard, new to his job and unarmed, had tried to wrest a shotgun from one of the bank thieves. The sheriff's eyes went directly to the set of ceramic tiles where Benji, a young man he had recommended for the job, had bled his life out through the hole of a shotgun blast.

Concentrating on the task at hand, Gonzalo noticed there seemed to be no one in the bank at all—not tellers, not customers, not managers. A split second of panic hit him. If the shooters had massacred a family, nothing would keep them from doing the same to the bank staff and patrons. At the end of the split second, a door creaked open and the bank manager's head peered out from a back office.

"Is everything clear?" the manager called out. Raul Mendez stepped out into the public area of the bank when he saw the sheriff waving to him.

"Where is everybody? Is the bank closed?" Gonzalo asked.

"We heard the shots and . . ." The manager's voice trailed off, and he looked down to his shoes as though they might better answer Gonzalo's questions. He had not been able to erase the memory of a half-dozen men with guns and bulletproof vests or of a bank guard shot dead.

"You had everyone go to the back? That's a very good strategy," Gonzalo said.

Of all the people in Angustias, he had the best sense of the bank manager's fears and worries associated with that horrible day. For the past two years he had shared them.

"I . . . I . . ."

Gonzalo put out a hand to stop Mendez from trying to justify his actions. He did not want the man to compound his fear with shame.

"I need to ask you a very specific question and I need an answer. Those men are in Angustias for a reason and it has to do with a great sum of money—possibly a million dollars. Has anyone deposited any large sums recently?"

"I'm not supposed to reveal . . ."

"I'm not asking you to tell me who, I just want to know if anyone has come here with a deposit of fifty thousand dollars or more."

"Yes."

"Okay. Now I need to know if it was anyone who would be surprising to me, someone we all think of as being poor."

"No. Nothing like that."

"Was it a lot more than fifty thousand dollars?"

Raul Mendez grew impatient as the workers and customers came out of the back offices and settled back into doing their business.

"Look, I'll tell you because I know you can get a warrant anyway. Martin Mendoza has made several very large deposits in the past two or three months. Hundreds of thousands. This is not so unusual for him. I think he might be liquidating some of his assets, but that is just my guess."

"Anybody else?"

"The lawyer, but not that much. Not fifty thousand dollars. She has won some cases recently, so I imagine this is her pay."

"And that's it?"

"Nobody else with any deposits in the range you were talking about."

Gonzalo bit his lip and thought for a moment.

"Thank you, Mendez. Don't tell anyone I asked these questions, okay?"

"Don't tell anyone I answered them."

Gonzalo started to walk away but turned back.

"These people you mentioned, did they make their deposits in cash or checks?"

"Checks."

"Thanks again."

Gonzalo went out through the glass doors of the bank and onto the plaza again, stopping there to stare for a moment at a dark cloud on the horizon. It would not be long before Angustias was under a deluge that would have been handy earlier that morning.

He continued on, walking to the house of Maria Garcia, the most successful lawyer in Angustias. Maria was still in her thirties, but she had already nearly run the other two lawyers in town out of business. They had never been able to match her attention to detail or her attention to the needs of her clients. They had been accustomed to doing business the old-fashioned way—waiting as long as possible to actually move on issues and telling clients what was good for them rather than letting the client define the goals of their work. She had been practicing law for several years, but one of her rival attorneys still chalked up each case she won in court and each new client she signed on to beginner's luck. The other said it was the short skirts she sometimes wore. Very few people cared anymore what these men said, however, and new business went to her.

Maria Garcia's house was one of those that lined the plaza. It had been tastefully restored to its late-eighteenth-century charm, but it was one of the few along the plaza that had been worked on recently and so it stood out from its neighbors somewhat. Gonzalo knocked on the door and after a minute or so of shuffling sounds, Maria opened it. She stood in a terry cloth bathrobe. She had the puffy eyelids of someone who had only been awake a short while or who desperately needed to get to bed.

"Just waking up?" Gonzalo asked.

"There was a damned lot of noise just a little while ago. Was that gunfire?"

She led the way into her living room. Gonzalo recognized the furnishings as replica art deco, a style he didn't particularly appreciate. He kept his critiques to himself. She sat cross-legged on a white sofa while Gonzalo remained standing.

"Yup, that was gunfire you heard."

"Great. One of the few days I take off from working, and people start shooting up the place. I can't get a full night's sleep in this town."

"It's afternoon," Gonzalo answered, more than a little surprised at the hours Maria Garcia chose for sleeping.

"You have no idea how much sleep I have to catch up on, Sheriff. Anyway, I assume nobody was hurt or you would be out there with them. Am I right?"

"Hector was shot. His bulletproof vest took the slug; he'll be okay. I'm here on a related matter. Counselor, have you been told about what happened to Pedro Ortiz?"

"Ortiz? Farmer?"

"That's the one. He and his wife were found dead this morning. His daughter was injured. I need to get information from you concerning—"

"He was murdered?" Maria Garcia held a hand to her lips, her eyes wide with disbelief.

"Yup. I wouldn't want to spread any rumors before I've finished my investigation, but if I can ask you a few questions . . ."

"He wasn't my client, Sheriff."

"Okay, I was hoping he was, but answer a different question. Has anyone come to you in the past few months with the dilemma of having too much money? Maybe someone who asked for advice about buying a house or other expensive property—someone we wouldn't think had any money?"

"Nope. Normally, I would tell you that was between me and my clients, but nobody comes even close to that description, Sheriff. My clients all come with the problem of having too little money, not too much. How much are we talking anyway?"

"A half million. Maybe a million."

Maria Garcia laughed at hearing the sum.

"Martin Mendoza is the only person who has anything like that kind of money, and what he has, he's had since he was born. You know that better than I do, Gonzalo. Why? What does this have to do with Ortiz?"

Gonzalo thought for a moment before answering. The pause lent weight to what he said.

"It seems Ortiz had this money I'm talking about, and the person shooting up the town would like to have it back. I'm guessing this guy is some drug lord. Anyway, he obviously hasn't found what he was looking for yet, and I'd like to find it first."

Maria Garcia twirled a lock of hair, thinking.

"First of all, drug lords don't run around small towns looking for loot. They send other people to do that for them. More importantly, I know a lot of the farmers of Angustias. I do business with many of them. The older ones don't use the bank, especially not since the shoot-out a while back. Some of these guys hide their money on the farm; they bury it. Is it possible Pedro Ortiz might have done something like that?"

"I doubt it. Two guys came to his house; they shot his daughter, they killed his wife, then they killed him. I figure, he would have told them where it was before letting his family get hurt."

"Ah, but then you didn't know him that well, did you?"

"I knew him as well as I know anyone else in Angustias," Gonzalo blurted out.

"He was mixed up in drugs, Gonzalo. You didn't know him as well as you thought. It's okay to admit that."

Maria Garcia stood up and went over to the bar she kept stocked with the finest rums of Puerto Rico along with a large assortment of other liquors. She took two ice cubes from a minifridge under the bar, poured out two inches of Don Q, and swirled the drink with a swizzle stick before drinking down half of it.

"Would you like some?" She motioned to Gonzalo with the glass in hand, but he shook his head.

"Ah, right. You're on duty," she said, and she took another sip.

Maria Garcia's drinking habits had scared Gonzalo when he first got to know her, but he had never seen her so much as tipsy. She was always clearheaded on the occasions when he consulted with her, and since she was one of the few lawyers in town and easily the most competent one, his interactions with her were frequent.

"You said, Ortiz, his wife, and his daughter were all shot, but didn't he have another child?"

"The little boy's with Mari, and the girl is at the clinic. I think I'll be able to locate some other family members soon, but first I've got to get this killer."

"Are the children in danger?"

"I don't think so. I think the wife was killed to get Pedro to talk. Pedro's not going to talk now no matter what."

Maria Garcia finished her drink and poured herself another sip. "It looks like I should get dressed and start looking into Ortiz's financial affairs."

"Why?"

"Who else is going to make sure that farm lands in the children's hands?"

"I see."

"Anything else I can help you with, Gonzalo? I've got to get going."

"Yeah. You're a lawyer. Tell me about Primavera."

"The mayor? What do you want to know?"

"Everything you can tell me in three minutes."

"Well, let's see. I know him from his time with the governor's office. He prepared briefs for court cases. He actually went to trial five or six times that I know of. Once against me. He was certainly competent."

"Did he beat you?"

"Well, remember, he was just part of a team."

"He won?"

"Oh, hell no. I stomped them. They settled for more than I had sued for. The administration wanted this problem to disappear."

"Tell me about the case."

"I'm sorry, Sheriff. I can't discuss the particulars of the case. Court order. You'd need another court order to release me from that obligation."

"Is that something I should do to help clear the Ortiz case?"

Maria Garcia finished her second drink. "I don't see a connection. If anything turns up, I'll let you know."

"Good. Now tell me about the people Primavera worked for."

"That will take more than three minutes, Gonzalo."

"I'll give you four."

CHAPTER TEN

Collazo made his way close to the burned-out house and stopped at the toolshed in back. He knew he had made good time and that the two young men in the car would not catch him if he paused for a moment or two. He wasn't tired, but he feared a confrontation without at least the semblance of a weapon in his hand. He didn't want to tell Calderon of a threat and not be able to help her combat it. He searched the shed for something he could wield. He hefted a mattock but thought again. He could not deny his eighty years; the tool was too heavy for him. He took a machete instead, testing the sharpness of the blade with a scrape of his thumb. Young Pedro had kept the machete as sharp as any Collazo had ever owned. He continued on toward the house and Officer Calderon.

By the time he got around to the front of the house, Officers Ramos and Jimenez were parked in front in their squad car, and

Calderon was talking to them through the passenger window. Collazo waved to them, but they were intent on their conversation and didn't see him until he reached their side.

"The guys in the Jeep were driving onto the Mendoza property. They had put the fence to one side and went through like they owned the place," Jimenez told Calderon.

"Did you get a good look at them?"

"It's a black Jeep. Two males, young—I don't recognize them, but that doesn't mean much. They didn't park right after they got on the property. It looked like they were going to keep driving on the land. They put up some branches to hide the entrance," Jimenez said.

"They're bad men," Collazo said, only a little winded.

Calderon turned to look at him.

"What makes you say that?"

"There's a track in the woods that leads out to the Mendoza land. They've been using it to get onto Pedro's territory. The tracks lead right up to the fence dividing the two properties. I think it's their drugs that were burned back there."

Officer Calderon stood up straight and arched her back, her hands on her hips. She was the senior officer at the scene and, though Jimenez and Ramos had never worked with Collazo, she was inclined to trust his view of the situation.

"Let's try to raise Gonzalo," she said. She waved her useless radio with its melted antenna to explain why she couldn't do this simple task herself.

Jimenez took hold of the CB and got only static. This was not unusual in Angustias. The mountains that made up most of the town's area blocked much of the radio communication unless one was on a summit and communicating with someone on another high point. Otherwise the valleys and folds of the mountains allowed radio contact along specific contour lines that took time and patience to learn. Though Calderon was not the most veteran of the officers, she had dedicated herself to solving the riddles posed by Angustias's hills. She thought about sending Jimenez and Ramos to the nearest point that would get them a clear line to Gonzalo, but then she thought better of it.

"Drive around to Mendoza's property and find out what these guys want. There's a chance they're connected with these murders so exercise some caution." Calderon could tell this last bit of information was almost insultingly obvious, but decided against apologies. Better safe than sorry.

Jimenez nodded, put the squad car in gear, and drove off.

Calderon turned her attention to Collazo. He spoke first.

"I think those men are coming here, child. I tell you they're connected to the murders, the drugs, everything. They're killers, cold-blooded."

"Okay, even if you're correct, what would you like me to do about it? I can't arrest them for murder when all they've done so far is trespass. In fact, I can't even arrest them for trespass. For all I know, they have permission from Mendoza to be on his property."

"We should leave. Hide in the woods and let them do what they want here."

"I can't do that, Collazo. You wouldn't do it if you were still an officer. . . ."

"You're wrong, child. Being an officer doesn't mean committing suicide."

The philosophical discussion was cut short by the arrival of the two men, subjects of the conversation. Calderon saw them as they made their way on foot through the mud around the right side of the house. The shorter one, with the sunglasses, smiled at Calderon and waved as though he were a visiting member of the family. Collazo was out of his field of vision for the moment. With a shift of her eyes and a slight change in posture, Calderon told Collazo to head around the left side of the house where he could hide. He did, his eyes pleading with her to follow his example.

"This is a crime scene, gentlemen," Calderon told the men as they neared. "I have to ask you to leave."

The men kept walking until they had come to within five feet of the officer. The taller one crossed his arms on his chest. The shorter man tilted his head to one side, smiled, and put his hands up with palms to the sky.

"We would be happy to leave, but we're looking for something, and we really can't leave without it."

Calderon was certain from his accent that the man who spoke was Dominican, not Puerto Rican, but that didn't really make any difference to her then.

"I'm sorry if you lost something here, but I have to insist." She put her right hand on the butt of the gun in her holster.

The smiling man put his hand to his heart and said, "I understand. I understand. You have a job to do, and you have to do it. I just hope you understand that I have a job to do, too, and I have to do it."

He turned away from her and stepped toward the house. Calderon took a step after him and reached out her right hand toward his shoulder. Before she touched him and without so much as a look back, he told the taller man, the man who didn't smile, "Kill her."

In one motion, the taller man pulled a gun from his rear waistband, aimed at Calderon's heart, and pulled the trigger. The impact of the bullet knocked Officer Calderon off her feet and onto her back in the mud. The gunman took two steps to stand over her.

Calderon would report later that she didn't remember falling to the ground, so the view she had, first of blue sky, then of the young man staring down at her, was particularly disorienting. She saw the barrel of a Beretta 9mm pointed at her face and tried to reach for her gun, but in confusion she used her left hand and pulled out her radio instead. The young man, seeing the move but not recognizing that there was no real threat, changed his aim and put a hole in the radio and a small nick on Calderon's left index finger.

At that moment, because of the ringing pain in her hand and because she recognized the need to put up a struggle of some kind, Iris Calderon started to turn onto her stomach. The move put her attacker off balance a bit, giving her just enough time to get onto her hands and knees. He regained his balance as she started to crawl away from him, and he followed.

The smiling man, on the Ramirez porch now, turned away from the scene. He didn't notice Collazo hurrying from the side of the house toward Calderon's assailant. The noise of gunfire tends to dull the sense of hearing so that the sound of an old man treading wet grass with courage is inaudible.

Calderon's attacker stood over her again and shot her between the shoulder blades, flattening her into the mud. He took a step to straddle her prone body, aiming carefully for the back of the head as she tried shakily to lift from the mire. It was in the split second before he would have pulled the trigger a fourth and fatal time that he felt the slash of Collazo's machete across his back. He yelled in pain and wheeled about, one hand holding the gun and the other reaching for the wound.

Collazo had struck the young man with a downward stroke. The machete's razor edge had struck bone at the right shoulder blade and cut deeply into muscle all the way across the man's back diagonally to the left hip. Had Collazo been any closer, he would have chopped into the man's neck, killing him. As it was, when the gun was wildly brandished in Collazo's direction, he parried with an upswing of the machete, slicing into the man's upper arm. The gun dropped, and the assailant stumbled backward over Officer Calderon's body and fell, clutching his injured arm to his chest.

"Hey! Grandpa!" the smiling man yelled. He had left the porch and was walking toward Collazo with a Beretta in his hand. He stopped ten feet from the old man and raised the weapon with one hand, holding it sideways with his head tilted to the opposite side in a stance he had seen in a dozen Hollywood productions.

"You going to die, Grandpa!"

He fired the weapon in Collazo's direction, hitting a coconut in its tree across the road, knocking it to the ground, bleeding milk. The young man pulled off two more shots; the bullets were never found. Collazo charged the man at this point with his machete raised over his head. The man turned and ran, slipping once in the mud at the side of the house and losing his gun. He got up and continued running without looking back or trying to recover the weapon.

Collazo pretended to give chase for a few steps but gave up, knowing he had no chance of catching a man one quarter his age even if he did insist on tripping over his own feet. Instead, he secured the gun from the mud, holding it by the trigger guard with a pinky.

When he turned back to Calderon and her assailant, the officer was motionless, facedown in the mud, but the criminal was holding his arm to his chest and inching along on the ground, nearing the gun he had dropped. Collazo rushed to his side. He raised the machete over his head with his free hand.

"¡ Quedate ai, condena'o, o te pesqueso!" he yelled. "Stay there or I'll chop your head off!"

The man stopped his struggles, and Collazo picked up his gun as well before stepping over to Calderon's side. He stabbed the tip of the machete into the clay earth and used it for support as he knelt beside her. He shook her by the shoulder, and she began to move.

"Are you in pain, child?"

Calderon tried to give an ironic look to show how ridiculous the question was when posed to a person who had just been shot twice, but her face only reflected the intense hurt that shocked through her torso with each subtle movement, including those necessary for the previously simple act of breathing.

"Stay down. Get your breath. That idiot's running toward Jimenez and Ramos. They'll get him. This one over here isn't going anywhere."

Collazo helped the deputy work her way to a sitting position. She leaned much of her weight on a hand splayed out on the grass behind her. She tried to unholster her gun but the hand shook violently, and she was unable to undo the snap.

"Rest, child. I'm here, and I've got two guns." Collazo held up the guns, and she tried to smile.

Jimenez and Ramos had entered Martin Mendoza's field using the same gate as the shooters, but they had gone in on foot. The beginning of the trail was filled with thick roots and heavily rutted by the torrential rains that sometimes hit the area. A Jeep was precisely the right vehicle to drive this road, but more experienced officers would probably have risked the damage to the squad car given the possibility of having to confront unforgiving killers.

The officers were within a hundred feet of the parked Jeep when they heard the three shots that hit Calderon. They were just far enough away to make them doubt they had heard anything significant at all, but the second set of shots, those aimed in Collazo's direction, decided the issue for them and they ran as quickly as they could through the tall grass to their squad car again. They got back on the road and made the short trip to where they had just left Calderon some minutes before, and they did not see when the smiling man, no longer smiling, drove off Martin Mendoza's property in his Jeep.

"What happened here?" was their first question as they got out of the squad car and jogged to Calderon's side.

Calderon's teeth were chattering, her breath was short, and her right arm shook. She was also developing a nearly incapacitating headache. She would have preferred to take two aspirins with a shot or two of Bacardi and curl up in a nice warm bed. She spoke in quick bursts.

"Cuff him. Take him to clinic. One stays with him. The other finds Gonzalo. Find other guy. With Jeep. Go."

"We should take you to the clinic, too, shouldn't we?"

Calderon shook her head. "I'm not riding with that thing," she said.

Collazo gave further instructions.

"Don't let him out of your sight—he tried to kill a cop, he killed two people here, and it's a drug case. If we give him to *los federales* he'll get the death penalty. He's desperate. Don't ask him any questions. Not even his name. Don't let him talk to anyone alone, not even the doctors. It's for their protection, too. He doesn't even go to the bathroom alone. You understand?"

Both men nodded and they cuffed the shooter, raised him to his feet between them, and walked him to the squad car. He had clearly lost a lot of blood; his pants were soaked with the blood and the wetness of the grass. As Jimenez opened the squad car door, the criminal made a halfhearted attempt to struggle free, but it took only a push from one of the officers to get him into the backseat of the car. They drove off with the sirens on though the road to the clinic was bound to be clear at this time of day.

"You see, *mi'ja*," Collazo said. "Things can run smoothly even while you're resting. Other people can do some of the work, and you don't have to worry about everything yourself."

"Did they pat him down?" she asked.

"What?"

"Did they check him for a second weapon?"

"I didn't notice."

"Damn," Calderon said, her teeth still chattering. "I should have thought of that."

CHAPTER ELEVEN

Two years prior to the Ortiz murders, the town of Angustias faced a tragic and harrowing set of incidents and overcame them. Barely. The group of thugs led by a corrupt cop from San Juan had attacked the bank and Gonzalo's family, shooting officers and civilians indiscriminately. When Angustias recovered from the initial shock of the attack, the citizens found that there were many people to blame and more than enough blame for each of them.

Gonzalo had been vilified by some in town because his investigation of the corrupt cop had brought about the murders and the heartaches. But then, he had suffered, too, and if he had brought about the problem, he had also shown himself to be part of the solution. He had arrested Nestor Ochoa, the corrupt cop, and he had brought about the downfall of other rotted law officers and minor political figures from across the island.

The mayor of Angustias had no excuses or explanations and his complete innocence in any wrongdoing did not satisfy most of his constituency. A town meeting he called two months after the attack turned into a shouting match. The mother of the slain security guard, for whom all rightly felt sympathy, had taken a microphone in hand to yell at the top of her lungs, *"¡Assesino! ¡Assesino!"* over and over until the crowd took up the chorus and Mayor Ramirez, for the first time in his life, retreated.

After the meeting, Ramirez had tried to make amends for sins he had not committed and for not preventing what he had had no part in bringing about. Ramirez was not, however, the man to make apologies that would satisfy anyone. As election time neared, Ramirez lost the will to campaign for the post he had served in for three terms. In the end, he seemed to say (and in fact was heard to say by several), "Vote for who you like. I don't care anymore." The people of Angustias did vote for who they liked, and they didn't like him. Instead they voted for Francisco Primavera.

The new mayor was young and handsome and unquestionably intelligent. Primavera was Angustias-born and -raised. His parents were poor like most parents in Angustias, but he had come in at the head of his class in high school, graduating with a perfect 4.0, earning a full-tuition scholarship to the state university. He attended the Río Piedras campus, studying political science; then he went to law school in New York City to perfect his English and make contacts. Primavera came back to Angustias summers and Christmas breaks to be with family and to argue politics with his aunts and uncles. In fact, he argued with people other than his relatives and it didn't have to be about politics. He was smarter than most and had the grades and degrees to prove it and the burning desire to make certain every citizen of Angustias knew it. They did.

While achieving his law degree, Francisco Primavera interned one summer with a justice of the Supreme Court of Puerto Rico. After the degree, he worked with the governor's office. When people asked why he hadn't taken a higher-paying position with a law firm in the States, he told them, "I want to make a difference," in a way that made them understand he thought they were failing in that department. After five years with the governor's office, he came back to live in Angustias, ran for mayor, and won.

Until the day of the murders, Gonzalo had never paid much attention to Francisco Primavera. As the chief law officer in Angustias, it was Gonzalo's job to pay attention to those youths that caused trouble. This did not leave much time for keeping tabs on those who excelled in school, worked hard, and did good. Gonzalo never paid the mayor much attention though he reported to him weekly about the petty crimes that happened in and around the small town. He never paid Primavera attention though he had recently hammered out a detailed budget plan with the mayor. He never paid Primavera attention, but like most of Angustias, he had voted for him. But what Maria Garcia had told him about the mayor and especially his connections to Puerto Rico's government made him realize that Primavera had to be watched.

Gonzalo stepped out onto the plaza after meeting with Garcia and looked around. It had turned into a beautiful afternoon. The rain clouds that had menaced earlier had found some other path and taken it. There was a warm breeze and a bird singing, obviously marking out his territory. Several of the older men in the town had congregated under the scant shade of one of the plaza trees as they often did. It was as though nothing had happened in the town that day; as though nothing had happened on the plaza less than an hour before. The town was too quiet. He knew there should have been at least an officer or two on patrol. Gonzalo went to his office to find out whether the mayor had called Naranjito. The town had a larger police force than Angustias and was always ready to lend a helping hand. He didn't think it would be wise to trust the mayor with even this routine and simple thing.

He called Sheriff Susana Ortiz of Naranjito. Ortiz was trustworthy, and Gonzalo could tell that his mayor had a crush on her. Which young man in Angustias didn't? Sheriff Ortiz had an easy disposition and a body that older men would term generous. She did nothing to hide her curves, and even a flak jacket looked good on her. When Ortiz became one of the first female squad commanders in Puerto Rico, a lot of the more *machista* officers on the force had harassed her—the old line about a woman taking away a job from men with families to support was often followed up with comments about her cleavage getting her the promotion and remarks far more crude. Gonzalo had been her first and staunchest supporter and a mentor. She felt she owed him a debt she could not repay, but the fact that she had cuffed Nestor Ochoa had Gonzalo feeling the situation was the reverse.

"What's happening up there, Gonzalo?"

"What have you heard?" Gonzalo answered.

"I'm hearing strange things about multiple homicides and shoot-outs."

"I'm sorry to say, it's all true. I was wondering whether you were able to send some of your officers to help with patrolling. We have two men on the loose here, and we could use the manpower, at least for a couple of hours."

"I can spare you, uh, let's see . . . Four officers, all good ones. Let me know if you need more than that, I can make a few phone calls and bring people in."

"No, no. Four would be great. I'll brief them when they get into town. I'll be somewhere between Pedro Ortiz's house and Rafael Ramirez's house—Kilometer One Point One and Three Point Nine on Route Seven Twenty-seven."

"Okay, got it. Anything else?"

"Yeah. Just out of curiosity, what exactly did Mayor Primavera tell you about our situation when he called you earlier?"

"Primavera? He never called. I heard rumors from two or three of your citizens. I've been waiting for you or Primavera to call. I was beginning to think it was all just *bochinche del barrio*—gossip. Why?"

"Oh, no reason."

"*A otro perro con ese hueso,*" Ortiz said, laughing—"Take that bone to another dog." She knew the workings of Gonzalo's mind better than most. "What's really going on here?"

"Let's say I have nothing concrete yet, but I think I'm putting something together. Maybe. We'll talk later, when I have something useful to say."

Gonzalo hung up the phone and rubbed his forehead with his right palm. The day had been long already and the sun wasn't down yet. He fished an aspirin bottle out of the lap drawer of his desk and swallowed two tablets; then he got up and took a sip of water in a little paper cone from the water cooler out of habit. He thought, as he balled up the cone, that the only thing that would make his headache disappear would be the sight of a certain Jeep overturned and burning with the occupants strapped in and roasted. He wondered for a moment whether such a thought was a sin. He decided he would confess it in a few weeks. First, he would get the bastards.

He went to put his hat on and saw that it was dirty and sweated all the way around the rim. He decided on wearing the department-issue baseball cap instead of his Smokey Bear.

"It looks good on you," Carlos said from his cell.

Gonzalo looked at his prisoner and thought about releasing him. He certainly didn't want to have to deal with Carlos if he ever caught the men in the Jeep. Carlos was a troublemaker and for hitting an officer he would certainly see some jail time, but he was also poor and friendless so he was no risk to flee Angustias, much less Puerto Rico.

"Tell me what happened out there," Carlos said while Gonzalo was deciding to keep him in custody.

"I'm busy, Carlos, and I have a headache."

"Yeah, I saw that with the aspirin, but maybe I can figure it all out for you, you know like that guy on TV."

"What guy?"

"The detective guy."

"Columbo?"

"No, the other guy, the old guy. They used to give his show, not anymore."

"Barnaby Jones?"

"That one."

"When I get some time, I'll tell you everything I know. Right now, I have to catch a killer."

"Who got killed?" Carlos asked, but Gonzalo was already halfway through the door and didn't stop.

At about the same time that Gonzalo was having his conversation with Carlos in the station house, Hector Pareda was pulling up in front of the Ortiz home. Iris Calderon was still sitting on the grass, Collazo standing next to her with the two retrieved guns lying on the ground at his feet.

"What happened here?" was, of course, Hector's first question as he knelt beside Calderon.

Iris's hands were still shaky, and she started to cry when she tried to answer him. Hector's breath came to him in hard quick bursts as he controlled a rage that was filling him, welling up within.

"Those *sin vergüenzas* with the black Jeep," Collazo said. "They came back through Mendoza's property. They came here telling

Calderon they were going to have a look around. When she told them they had to leave, the smiling one, the darker-skinned guy, he told the bigger one, 'Kill her,' just like that, like it was nothing, like killing a bug . . ."

"Where were you?" Hector turned on his old partner.

"I was where she told me to be, son. She said to go around to the side of the house. I went."

"And you let them shoot her?"

"They shot her twice—"

"And what did you do?"

It was clear to the old man that Hector was accusing him of cowardice, but Collazo was not the man to react to such an accusation. He had learned in his many years, including many as a law officer, that people will say anything and turn on anyone when anger overflows. Iris Calderon intervened, pulling on Hector's sleeve and keeping him from continuing a confrontation he would only be ashamed of later.

"He saved my life, Hector," she said. Her lips were still trembling and her voice was not strong. "Collazo almost killed the man who shot me. He chased away the other man. I owe Collazo everything."

Hector felt the shame Iris wanted to avoid. He drew her close to his chest, and she could tell that he was crying into her hair. As he drew away from her, she noticed the bullet hole in his shirt.

"You got shot?"

"Same guy. It was a grazing wound; the vest took it all. I'll just have a bruise."

Hector stood up and looked off into the mountains, thinking; then he looked to Collazo.

"He said, 'Kill her'? Where is he?"

"He got by Jimenez and Ramos. Who knows where he is now? The other guy is in the clinic," Collazo answered.

Hector was silent, but fury was written into every crease of his face. He was the senior deputy at the scene now, and he wanted to think like he was under control and in charge of his emotions and the situation, but he wasn't. He wanted to give an order, but the only course of action that seemed reasonable was for him to drive to the clinic and get information from the injured assailant, probably through the use of the nightstick or the pistol. He would ask, "Where's the smiling guy?" with a gun to the injured man's head, and, when he had been told what he wanted to hear, he would pull the trigger. This seemed like the best thing to do, but he knew there was a flaw in the plan somewhere. He just couldn't see it.

Hector turned to Collazo. The old man could see the tears in Hector's eyes.

"Do you want me to tell you what to do?" Collazo asked softly, so softly that Iris couldn't hear him. Hector nodded.

"Give me your car keys, and I'll take the girl to the clinic. You watch the site for a little while. Maybe you can dust these guns for fingerprints while you wait. I'll come right back with the car and you can drive off and do your work. How does that sound?"

Hector nodded again. The plan did sound better in some way he couldn't then explain. He knelt beside Iris again and kissed her lips.

"Go with Collazo," he told her and helped her stand and walk to his squad car.

Collazo got into the driver's seat while Hector got the print kit from the trunk. The older man waved as he drove away, and he watched Hector through the rearview mirror. The younger man stood in utter dejection.

This is why they don't let cops fall in love with their coworkers, Collazo said in his mind, but he said nothing aloud because it wasn't his place.

Back in the center of town, Gonzalo walked to his car. He drove off to meet with Rafael Ramirez, the former mayor of Angustias.

As he pulled away from the station house, the young smiling man, covered in mud, was walking into the *alcaldia* for a second meeting with the mayor. This one would be as short as the one earlier in the day.

The young man strode confidently down the hallway leading to the mayor's office door and pushed it open hard enough to make it bounce off the small, decorative table placed behind it. Primavera jumped to his feet at this intrusion and Miguel Belen, who had been leaning over the mayor's desk with his palms flat on the surface, stood upright and crossed his arms.

"Call your boss," the young man yelled at the mayor.

"Who do you want me to call? The chief of police? The governor?" Primavera yelled back.

The young man lifted a finger at the mayor, coming close to him, menacing him.

"I don't care who you call. You're going to have a big problem here. I guarantee it. Your people just sliced up my partner bad. If he dies, there's going to be hell to pay. Anyway, the boss lost a million dollars in this town today. Don't think that's going to go away."

"Look, what's your name?"

"Fidel Castro."

"Okay, whatever. Look, your best move is to get out of my office and get out of my town. Officers are coming."

"Give me a gun," Fidel said.

The mayor looked to his deputy mayor. Miguel Belen shrugged, and the young man, whose name really was Fidel Castro, shouted his demand again with a hand outstretched. Primavera opened the lap drawer of his desk and brought out a small handgun. He offered it butt-end first to Fidel.

"Don't give me that little popgun; I've got work to do."

With that, Fidel walked over to a chair in a corner of the room and picked up a pump-action shotgun that was lying across the arm-rests. He pumped a shell into the chamber and smiled.

"Call your boss," he tossed over his shoulder as he walked out, and the mayor put his handgun back into its drawer.

CHAPTER TWELVE

Gonzalo sat on a rocking chair on Rafael Ramirez's front porch. He didn't want to sit . . . he wanted to stand and ask questions and have them answered. He had officers who might be in danger and he had to get back into the field to lead them. Still, Rafael Ramirez was in no mood to be bossed or hurried, and he hadn't been in such a mood since being replaced as mayor of the town.

Ramirez came out to the porch with a glass of soda, a paper towel wrapped around it to sop up the sweat of the glass. He handed this to Gonzalo and sat himself on a rocking chair.

"I'm planting peppers," he said as Gonzalo took a sip of the soda.

"I have people being murdered in this town," Gonzalo answered. He would have liked to have had time for tact.

"Do you want me to join a posse?" Ramirez said, and Gonzalo

could tell he was beginning to be upset. "Or would you like me to start praying for the dead?"

"I'd like you to give me a little help, just a little information."

"A little information? I don't know anything that Primavera doesn't know, Gonzalo."

"Maybe not, but he's a little hard to talk to right now. . . ."

"Tell me about it. He more or less told me to go to hell."

"Well, I need to know what you can tell me about him."

Ramirez stopped the motion of his rocking chair and looked down at his shoes for a moment. He was trying to figure out what he was missing in understanding a question that made no sense to him.

"Gonzalo, you know as much about him as I do. You probably know more."

"But I don't know the right pieces of information."

"I'll tell you what I know."

"Talk to me about his political connections. Explain his relationship with the governor's office and with his party."

"Ah, that I can talk about," Ramirez said, and he did.

Emilio Collazo entered the clinic, the only clinic in Angustias, with his arm around Iris Calderon. She had trouble keeping her steps in a straight line. Her legs were shaky and once she got into the sitting position in the squad car, it was hard for her to get up again.

Collazo expected to find the clinic in a bustle, but it was calm. Deputy Jimenez was conversing with Dr. Perez, the clinic's chief practitioner, in a low voice and averted his eyes when he saw Collazo. When Perez noticed Calderon, he rushed to her side and took her off Collazo's hands. Jimenez was left with Collazo, and the older man, noticing the deputy's discomfort, started conversation.

"Where's your partner?"

"In the bathroom; he should only be another minute."

Body language told Collazo that Jimenez thought that even a minute was too long to wait. He couldn't understand the anxiousness.

"How's the criminal?" he asked.

"Uh, well, the doctor's gonna want to talk to you about that, I think."

"Why? I can't help him fix anything."

"I don't think there's anything to fix."

"Are they all done with him?"

"Yeah. I think you can say that."

At that moment, Officer Ramos emerged from the bathroom and Jimenez was glad to be able to take his leave with a nod and a weak smile.

"We've got to get back on the road," Ramos said.

"Get back to the Ortiz property first," Collazo suggested to them, not certain that they knew how to do their jobs.

The two men went out to the parking lot, and Collazo took a seat in the waiting area. There were two other patients at the moment, both children with their mothers. He waved and nodded to them, but the children were more interested in toys they had brought with them and their mothers were reading and only smiled back at him. He availed himself of a magazine on the seat next to his, but its cover advertised forty foolproof ways to please your man, and he put it down without opening it. It was only a couple of minutes before Dr. Perez came out to the waiting area and motioned to him.

"How's the girl?"

"Officer Calderon will be fine. I've given her a mild sedative to calm her shakes. I've visually and palpably examined her back and ribs, and I don't think there are any breaks. We'll take an X ray to be positive. I will give her the option of staying overnight."

Perez was a transplant to Angustias who remained aloof from the citizens though he served them well and faithfully and had done so for many years. He was tall and thin, thinner than Collazo, with a thick head of hair that was beginning to recede. In the years Collazo had known him, he had never seen him out of the thick-rimmed glasses that he wore now along with a white lab coat that almost reached his knees.

"Don't ask her if she wants to stay," Collazo said. "Tell her she has to."

"Well, I can't really do that, Deputy, but I'll strongly suggest it. With the amount of bruising she shows, it would be wise if she stayed under our care."

"Tell her she can stay here until she's relieved at least; someone has to look after the prisoner."

"Actually the prisoner died."

"Are you sure?"

"It's not that hard to figure out," Dr. Perez said, not sure how else to respond. "I've already called for his body to be picked up. It'll probably be an hour or so. Hopefully not longer. We don't have the facilities for him here."

"What happened to him? I mean, what killed him?"

"He bled to death."

Collazo put a hand to his lips, losing himself in thought.

"The wound on his arm cut through a small artery," the doctor explained, gesturing to his own arm to outline the wound and the course of the artery.

"I didn't see any spurting," Collazo said.

"Well, neither did I at first. The spurting was muzzled by his flesh and his shirt. It looked like just heavy seepage, but he had lost a lot of blood at the scene and in the car, and he continued to lose blood here. It was probably already too late for him when they put him in the car. Anyway, we tried, but he didn't make it." The doctor shrugged.

Collazo thought for a few seconds.

"Did he say anything? Any personal effects in his pockets?"

"The patient said nothing at all. He was hardly conscious when I saw him. I personally emptied his pockets. He had forty-three dollars and seventy-seven cents and a set of keys. They're in a bag in my office."

"No ID?"

"None."

Collazo put out his hand after another moment of thought. He was shaken by the news that he had killed a man. He was questioning whether he had needed to swing so hard into the man's arm with the machete. An ounce of restraint would have spared the man's life and, not unimportantly, it would have preserved a suspect for interrogation. Dr. Perez took Collazo's hand and shook it, taking him out of his reverie.

"Do you want to see the body before you go? Maybe you can find something on him that might be useful? He has tattoos, a few old scars . . ."

Collazo didn't really want to see the body—he had seen people he had killed before, and the experience never felt good—but he followed the doctor anyway. He felt he owed his victim at least that much.

The young man was on a gurney, under a sheet in an examining room. Perez pulled back the sheet revealing the man's head and torso. Collazo stepped close and peered down at the man's face; he whispered a promise that he would pray for his soul but he added in an even lower voice that he wasn't sure that would be enough to help him any.

"Do you want to see the tattoos?" Dr. Perez asked.

"No," Collazo answered. "I'll tell one of the deputies to do that or Gonzalo if I see him. I'm retired."

Collazo walked out to the car in the parking lot and looked up to the sun before getting in; it was just beginning to fade. He reflected that it was lucky for the people of Angustias that he had only become a deputy later in life. If he had been an officer early on, he might have had a chance to kill everyone. He got in the car and shook his head clear of the thought. It wasn't going to be of any help.

Gonzalo watched from the porch of Rafael Ramirez's house as officers from Naranjito drove past in two squad cars and pulled over a little farther down the road. They backed up and the passenger in each unit got out and walked over.

"You guys having a little trouble?" one of them asked.

"You could say that," Gonzalo answered. "I need two of you to stay in the center of town, near the *alcaldia*. Patrol on foot a little, make yourselves visible. The other car can go driving back and forth throughout the territory, visit the elementary school, the clinic, Colmado Ruiz, and the Ortiz home, that's just up the road a couple of kilometers—it's still smoldering so it shouldn't be hard to find. Do you know where everything else is?"

The officers looked at each other and nodded in the affirmative to Gonzalo. Sheriff Ortiz ran a good precinct and the officers under her were capable men and women. Gonzalo gave them a last bit of information and advice.

"Nobody goes solo on this. The man we're looking for is armed and extremely dangerous. He's too stupid to be afraid. He's driving around in a black Jeep. He's young, with short hair, a deep tan, a white T-shirt with the sleeves cut off. He had on shades. If you see him, don't let him out of your sight and don't approach him alone."

"You want us to shoot him on sight?" one of the officers joked.

"I wouldn't cry if you did," Gonzalo answered. "If you think you see him, have your gun out. He's not here for a social visit." Gonzalo pointed to the dried blood on his face. "He won't have any trouble shooting you down if he gets a chance."

The officers sobered, and Gonzalo and Ramirez watched them return to their cars.

"Well, Gonzalo, do you have the information you needed?" Ramirez said, breaking their silence.

"I'm not sure I have everything, but I have a lot to go on for now. If I think of any other questions, I'll come back out here."

"Why don't you just call?"

Gonzalo finished the last of his soda and put his cup on a small round glass-top table that sat between himself and the former mayor.

"I would miss the Pepsi," he said. Ramirez didn't smile. "Can I use your phone for a minute?"

"Long distance?"

"No. I want to call home."

The answering machine came on at his house and he called his mother's house next, which was only a few hundred yards away from where he thought Mari would be. She picked up the phone.

"How are things?" Gonzalo asked.

"Everything is fine over here. Your mother's been talking up a storm."

Gonzalo's mother had suffered a stroke during the attack on Angustias two years earlier and speech was often difficult for her, as was walking and any number of activities that had been effortless before.

"What about?"

"Oh, she's been telling Sonia all about you when you were a kid. I didn't know you ate roaches."

"One roach," Gonzalo answered. It felt good to fall into easy banter. He decided right then that the day had been too long for him, and as soon as the *Metropolitanos* arrived on the scene, he would give them as much control of the situation as they wanted. They always wanted total control, and today that would be fine with him. He had a family to share a life with, and he was tired.

"How was the little boy? Is he still with you?" Gonzalo asked, speaking of the youngest Ortiz.

"I left him with the clinic. A nurse knew of some family he had in a town nearby. They made the phone calls, and his relatives picked him up. He's young," Mari said. "He won't remember this day."

"Yeah, he won't remember any of this mess. I don't think he's even a year old. Anyway, say hi to Sonia for me. Let me see, it's . . . one-thirty now. I'm going to try to be home by six and have a quiet dinner until seven."

"You want to eat at your mother's house?"

"That sounds good to me. Give me a call if you want me to bring anything."

"Your mother has food for a month here, don't worry, Luis. Just do me one favor, okay?"

"What?"

"Come home in one piece."

Gonzalo made the promise and left Ramirez's house. He let Ramirez know he was going to check on the Ortiz property, then head over to the station house to follow up on the information on Primavera.

In his car, he looked at the few notes he had made during his conversation with the former mayor. Most of the information was uninteresting, but there had been a few people Ramirez had mentioned who had worked with or supervised Primavera that Gonzalo knew had been linked to minor scandals with the administration of the previous governor. Some, Gonzalo knew, were still working in government, while one or two had been forced to resign or, he wasn't sure, might actually be in prison. A few phone calls would put straight in Gonzalo's mind what involvement, if any, his current mayor had with the corrupt. First, the Ortiz house, he told himself as he put the car in gear—then make the phone calls.

CHAPTER THIRTEEN

Collazo was not overly surprised to find Hector still at the Ortiz home. Hector should have gone into town or consulted with Gonzalo, but he sent Jimenez and Ramos away instead. Collazo knew that though he looked calm at the moment, Hector was at the Ortiz home with only one hope. He wanted the other criminal to come back while he was there. He wanted the man in the Jeep to wave a gun and make demands. He was hoping for the confrontation. Collazo also knew that if the confrontation came, Hector would not hesitate, and he would not miss.

Collazo slowed as he approached the Ortiz house. His former partner was in front talking to a neighborhood boy of ten or twelve years of age. Hector mussed the boy's hair, and the child sprinted away as Collazo parked on the grass.

"Did he have anything useful?" Collazo asked, walking over to

Hector slowly. He was strong for his age, but the day was beginning to wear him down.

"Pablito? He wanted to know if he could take a look inside. I told him to come back when he's a cadet at the police academy, then we'll let him see all the dead people, burned-out houses, and crime scenes he could ever want to see."

"What did he say to that?"

"He can't wait," Hector answered. "Anyway, how's Iris?"

"They're going to try to hold her for observation, Perez said. I told him to keep her even if she insists that she's okay. Getting shot twice, even with the vest on, is serious, especially at that range. Her nerves are a wreck . . ."

Collazo stopped when he saw that Hector could not stand to hear discussion of Iris's condition. The younger man turned away briefly to clear something from his eye. He stayed turned away, and Collazo knew that the tears would not stop coming. He put an arm across Hector's shoulders.

"It's all right, son. I understand how you feel."

"No you don't," Hector said without turning back to Collazo. "I love her."

"You think I don't love?" Collazo asked.

"Did your wife ever get shot?" Hector answered.

"Cristina? No. But one day I'll tell you about my first wife. Losing her was hard, Hector. Very hard."

In his years of working with Collazo, Hector had never heard that Cristina was not the older man's first and only wife. He knew they had been married for half a century or more. He considered his words more carefully. He wiped his eyes again as well as his nose and turned back to Collazo.

"I want to apologize for—"

"Don't. It was nothing," Collazo answered. "The heat of the moment. Just believe me, I wanted her to abandon her post. Outgunned, I think she should have retreated as soon as we heard that the two guys were coming. No difference. She's brave and decided to make her stand. I wasn't going to run, Hector."

Hector nodded. "I know."

The men were silent for a minute or more. Collazo spoke. "Does Gonzalo know?"

Hector looked to his friend and gave him a smile that said the sheriff did not know and didn't have to know either.

"He's going to figure it out sooner or later, son. He is a pretty good detective," Collazo said.

"Let it be later then. Me and Iris are just getting to know each other. We've just started."

"You mean it might not last?"

"It'll last if I have anything to do with it," Hector said. "I can't get enough of her . . ."

Collazo held up one hand to stop his friend from going into any detail. He was a strict Catholic, and though he understood that Iris and Hector were of an age to make any choices they wanted about their relationship, it would hurt his image of them if he knew they were having sex.

"No, it's not like that Collazo. We're not doing anything to be ashamed of; I respect her too much and she respects herself. She's just . . . she's just the greatest person I know. I want to spend my days with her."

Collazo eyed his friend and smiled at his earnest tone. He had known Hector many years and through many of his relationships with women. Hector had never struck him as a man to settle down. Not that he was a womanizer in any way; he just didn't seem stable somehow—he was impulsive, and that picture of Hector simply didn't match with the Hector who made declarations of love and wanting to spend his life with one woman.

"You saved me, Collazo," Hector said, breaking the silence. "If I had gone with her to the clinic, I would have killed her shooter. I know it. I'd burn in hell for it, but I'd have done it with a smile."

"And it wouldn't have done you any good, Hector. You understand that, don't you? It wouldn't have helped Iris even a little bit."

"It wouldn't have been about helping Iris," Hector said. "It would have made me feel good."

"I bet it wouldn't. Anyway, try to put away your selfishness—the world, this job, your purpose on earth is not all about you."

"Don't start getting wise, Collazo."

The older man shrugged. "Anyway," he said. "The gunman died. I killed him. He bled to death."

Hector looked closely at his former partner, trying to tell whether Collazo was joking, but this was no joke. Collazo rarely joked and never about killing someone. Hector put an arm around him. At heart, Collazo was a gentle man who would carry the death of this criminal like a scar.

Collazo patted Hector on the shoulder, letting him know it was time to release him and put emotionalism aside.

"Do you feel better knowing the guy is dead?" Collazo asked. Hector had to acknowledge that the news did nothing to help him.

"Told you. Loving Iris can do you good. Hating, hurting, killing, revenge—none of that does any good. Believe me."

"If Gonzalo finds out about me and Iris . . ."

"He'll probably try to get her to go to another precinct."

"What am I supposed to do?"

"You're supposed to keep it quiet, especially in front of your superiors," Collazo said, nodding toward Gonzalo as he pulled up in front.

"Anything?" the sheriff asked.

"Did Ramos and Jimenez find you?" Hector responded.

"Nope."

"Well, boss, then you're in for one hell of an update."

Hector had Collazo report to Gonzalo about the attack on Officer Calderon and the death of the gunman. Gonzalo shared information about the officers from Naranjito who were helping, but he kept quiet about his suspicions concerning the mayor. He said only that he had phone calls to make and that he wouldn't be sorry if the remaining killer left town and never came back.

"There are thousands of police on this island. Let one of them catch him," he said. "I'm tired."

As he said this, two squad cars from the *Metropolitanos* drove past, ignoring the Angustias squad cars on the grass and the still-smoking house that clearly marked the crime scene they were headed for. The three men watched the *Metropolitanos* go by; then they looked at each other.

"Can you believe those guys? What do they think they were sent out here for?" Hector asked no one in particular.

"I didn't see a detective in the bunch," Gonzalo said. He started to walk to his car. "I'd better catch up with them. I'll get Jimenez to baby-sit the house," he told Hector.

"Anything you want me to do?" Collazo called after him.

"Go home," Gonzalo answered from the driver's seat; then he drove away.

Though it was mid-July, and only two-fifteen in the afternoon, the sun was beginning its descent. Unlike most of the United States, Puerto Rico doesn't bother to spring forward or fall back every six months. It would be dark at seven-thirty. The valleys were already taking on a twilight tinge because of the foliage overhead and the shadows of the mountains. Gonzalo drove slowly back to the center of town; he wanted to think about his injured officer and how Angustias was going to make it through the night even with the help of the officers from Naranjito and the big city police. He sighed to think that he would have to continue searching for the black Jeep and its driver until he was sure they were gone. The forests were so dense in so many parts of Angustias that a tractor trailer couldn't be seen from the air; on the ground you would almost have to walk right into the thing to notice it. First order of business, he told himself, was to organize his forces and conduct a search of every nook and cranny. Before he could do that, he had to figure out what his forces consisted of. Could he call Sheriff Molina of Comerio and have a few more officers sent his way? Could he deputize a few trusted citizens? Could he count on the *Metropolitanos* to send more people? It was, after all, a double homicide. He also needed to have a long talk with Francisco Primavera. No. First, he had to make the phone calls. No. Wait. First, he had to contact the *Metropolitanos* that had just arrived and fill them in. No. Wait . . . He was glad to enter town and park in front of the station house. He looked at his watch as he walked up to the door. He needed just five minutes of peace, he told himself, to make sense of his list of priorities.

As soon as he walked in, Carlos hopped off his bunk and came to the bars. Gonzalo rolled his eyes.

"They killed Ortiz and his family?" Carlos asked. His hands were holding onto the bars.

"Yup. How'd you know?"

Carlos pointed to the bars of his window. The window was a bit higher than a normal window, but the conversation of people walking on the sidewalk beneath it would be easily audible.

"They killed Ortiz, his wife, they burned his house down. That's all I can tell you right now."

"And that shoot-out on the plaza?"

"Go home, Carlos," Gonzalo said, fishing for the cell-door keys. He found them and opened up. Carlos was reluctant to step out.

"Go home. Stay in your house. Don't drink anything. I'll come by and get you tomorrow. I'm going to call Ruiz. I'll tell him that if he sells you a drink or a bottle, I'll arrest him, so don't even bother, okay?"

"You got murderers out there? I think I'd be safer in here," Carlos said.

"Yeah, maybe, but I don't want you here right now, so go."

Carlos stepped out hesitantly.

"It's a long walk to my house," he said.

"Then you'd better hurry," was Gonzalo's reply.

"I had money with me when I was brought in," Carlos said hopefully.

"You're still under arrest, Carlos, now get out before I hit you with something."

Carlos shuffled out the station house door leaving Gonzalo to his five minutes of peace at last. In that time, Gonzalo was able to figure out an order of events that needed to happen. If he worked hard, he could have dinner with his family. First, he needed to talk with the *Metropolitanos* that had driven into town. Strangely, they hadn't come to the station house. They might have gone to the *alcaldia* first. After talking with them, he would need to organize his remaining forces to conduct a thorough search of the many roads that crisscrossed the territory of Angustias including the abandoned farms and half-built houses. If the killer thought there was a million dollars hiding somewhere, he wouldn't be leaving until it was in his possession.

Then there would have to be a round of phone calls concerning Francisco Primavera followed by a talk with the mayor. Ramirez had given Gonzalo a bunch of names—people Primavera had worked with; several had been crooked one way or another, and though none were criminal masterminds, Gonzalo totaled them up and saw a half-dozen things Primavera might be guilty of. He looked at his watch and decided that he needed to take just a few minutes more to see if any of that crookedness might link back to what happened at the Ortiz house that morning. He rested his elbows on his desk and covered his eyes in "see no evil" fashion, trying to concentrate, but there was a double knock on the station house door, which opened immediately after. Two blue-uniformed officers walked in.

"Hey, Sheriff . . . uh"—the older one looked at his notepad—

"Sheriff Gonzalo. You called a few hours ago for some detective work?"

Gonzalo didn't stand to greet them. He quickly looked them over instead.

The one who had spoken was in his forties; he wore captain's bars on his shoulders. He was probably near to six feet in height and only the bulk of the bulletproof vest under his uniform shirt made him look anything more than medium in build. The man who followed after him was a sergeant, maybe in his late twenties and closer to five and a half feet tall. The bulk of his vest made his belly look less round, more angular than it was.

"Captain Guillermo Montalvo." The older man offered his hand, and Gonzalo got up and shook it. "This is Sergeant Rivera." He thumbed at the younger man, who also offered his hand for a shake.

"You're detectives?" Gonzalo asked, eyeing the blue uniforms.

"We've been on the street all day. Protests. Students came out of the Río Piedras campus to block traffic. We mobilized everyone to make sure that's all they did. I must have processed twenty disorder-lies myself."

"How many students were out there?"

"It looked like all of them. Anyway, we're here to work the case. If you can fill us in on where you are with all this, we can get down to business."

"Ah, okay. I thought you guys had forgotten all about us."

"Well, to tell the truth, Sheriff, we weren't sure we were going to make it, but we heard a cop got shot, so it became a priority."

That a double homicide might have been relegated to something that could wait seemed a bit strange to Gonzalo, but the detective smiled openly and Gonzalo took him at his word. He talked the men through what had happened earlier in the day, all the details of the shoot-out in town, and the attack on Officer Calderon.

"How's she doing?" Captain Montalvo asked. There was genuine concern in his face and voice.

"I understand she'll be fine, but I haven't had a chance to go see her yet," Gonzalo answered. "I've been pretty busy running around."

"No need to explain, Sheriff. We know you're stretched thin, that's why we brought along a couple of uniforms. We've spoken to the guys from Naranjito. My guys are out and making themselves visible. I think the first order of business has to be finding this black Jeep guy. Maybe if we can get all the available men to do a complete search of Angustias . . ."

"That's exactly what I was thinking. I can help you two while the four from Naranjito and your other two join two of my men in the field, looking under every rock."

"Maybe you can deputize two or three of your more capable citizens, just to act as eyes and ears, not to confront anyone . . . ," Montalvo continued.

"I've thought of that. I've got a few people I can trust for something like this."

"Good, good. Now you say that one of the perpetrators is dead in the clinic, right?"

"Yes."

"Okay, so what we'll do is let you make the calls to those potential deputies and organize the search parties while we take a look at the crime scene, collect some evidence, take a look at the corpses, and see what's what. How's that sound?"

Gonzalo agreed and shook hands again with Captain Montalvo. He had never thought that giving up control of an investigation would be so easy, but it felt like a burden of a thousand pounds had been lifted off his shoulders. Finally, there was help—a critical mass of law enforcement in the town, and he could see that the black Jeep driver would soon be trapped if he had decided to stay in Angustias.

"Meanwhile," Montalvo continued. "I see you have a fax that came in. Anything relevant to the case?"

Gonzalo noticed the curled paper hanging from the machine. He went over, tore it off, and skimmed it quickly before sharing with the detectives.

"They found a match for some prints we sent in from the crime scene," he said, showing them the paper.

"Daniel del Valle. Twenty-three years old," Montalvo read out. "Petty larceny, grand larceny, assault, assault, assault, assault, assault with a deadly weapon."

There was a blurred mug shot, black and white, mostly black, at the top of the sheet.

"Is this the guy in the Jeep?" Montalvo asked.

"That's the guy dead in the clinic."

"Look at the known acquaintances," the sergeant spoke out, pointing to one name. It was the first time Gonzalo had heard him speak. His voice was high-pitched, almost as though it had never dropped. Gonzalo took a second to recover from his surprise.

"Fidelio Castronueves? Aka Fidel Castro? He hangs out with the president of Cuba; who would have guessed? No wonder he's a screwup," Montalvo said.

"I'll call San Juan and see if I can get any further information on Castro; he might be the one we're looking for," Gonzalo said.

"Okay, later me and Sergeant Rivera will give a call to our home office. Del Valle was from our area; maybe we can get more about him and accomplices. First, the crime scene."

The detectives took their leave and drove off. Gonzalo got on his phone to call up first San Juan for information on Castro, then several of his most trusted *Angustiados,* to help out with the door-to-door search.

CHAPTER FOURTEEN

Jorge Nuñez agreed to be deputized and to go out searching for the black Jeep and its driver. He would carry a walkie-talkie, which he knew from experience would only work if it felt like it. Everyone else on Gonzalo's A-list, people who had been deputized before, backed out. It was three o'clock and a door-to-door search would take hours. Besides, this was no car vandal or shoplifter hiding in the woods; this was a cold-blooded killer of men, women, and children. Many had seen the city squad cars and the officers from Naranjito. If these police couldn't handle the situation, then the citizens of Angustias were better off not stepping out into what could be the line of fire.

Gonzalo made a few calls to a B-list he had in mind, but there were no takers there either, and after three or four rejections, he gave up. The whole town mustered one person willing to risk himself. Even Rafael Ramirez had declined the honor of hunting a murderer in the forests. Gonzalo thought about asking Collazo to get back to work, but decided against it. His friend had done enough.

Next, he started on phone calls to ask about the mayor's San Juan connections. Two phone calls to acquaintances in the San Juan police and two to low-level government officials Gonzalo knew turned up nothing incriminating about the connections. Each call provided him with a few more names to inquire about. The only interesting thing about the conversations he had was that though the people he spoke to knew more about Primavera's San Juan days than either Gonzalo or Rafael Ramirez, none of them said anything to clear the mayor of anything. Gonzalo got the impression that Primavera had been a yes-man in San Juan, going along with whatever seemed right to his superiors. This was despicable in its way, but then Primavera had been a young man, still was, and nothing tied him to the drug trade, or Daniel del Valle, or Fidel Castro.

Gonzalo jotted down the extra names he had collected and tried to put a relevant note next to each one for further review. He tore the sheet out of his notepad and locked it into his lap drawer. If the mayor came in or asked to review the notes of the case, there was no need for him to see that he himself was the subject of some investigation.

Gonzalo stood up and stretched. It was now nearing four o'clock. He wanted to check in with the mayor, Maria Garcia, and Iris Calderon before checking in with Hector to see how the search was going and with the detectives to ask if they'd found anything relevant. Then he wanted to eat. He hadn't had lunch yet. He walked out and around to the *alcaldia*.

The plaza in front of the government building was deserted. Gonzalo went up the steps and through the double doors. He went into the mayor's office without knocking. Inside, Primavera was speaking in hushed tones with his deputy mayor. He stopped with his arms raised, reaching around his neck, fixing the collar of the sports jacket he had just put on.

"Doesn't anyone knock in this town?" Primavera asked.

"Sorry. Would you like me to go out and try again?" Gonzalo was only half joking.

Primavera thought about the offer for a minute before asking what Gonzalo wanted.

"I'm here to update you on the investigation," Gonzalo said, a bit annoyed at having to state what should have been obvious.

"I thought that was being handled by the *Metropolitanos*."

"Well, they're here, but I'm working with them. Besides, I'm your main contact. This is how it works."

Primavera looked Gonzalo over. It was clear to the sheriff that his mayor didn't appreciate being told how things worked in the town that he ran. Gonzalo also got the feeling that the mayor wanted him off the case. He didn't have to speculate about this for long.

"Why don't you go home and let them take care of this? They have the equipment, the training."

"Are you headed home?" Gonzalo asked.

"As a matter of fact, yes I am. I need to eat something. I spoke with Detective Montalvo and he looks very competent. Go home, Gonzalo. There will be other cases. In fact, don't you have that guy who assaulted Officer Calderon?"

"I sent him home. I'll pick him up again tomorrow."

Primavera eyed him with suspicion again. "Okay. Then you really have nothing at all to do. Go home. Remember, you have a plane to catch tomorrow."

Gonzalo didn't show it, but he had forgotten that he was starting a vacation and would be in Paris with his wife and youngest daughter, Sonia, in thirty-six hours. They were going to meet his oldest daughter, Julia, who was working for an American company there, and his middle daughter, Laura, who was studying in Italy for the summer but would make the trip especially for the reunion.

"That's a good reason for me to get as much done as possible before I leave."

"Okay, do whatever pleases you. I'm going home. There are professionals here, trained to do the job."

Primavera started clearing papers off his desk, putting some in various drawers and others in an open briefcase he had resting on his seat.

Gonzalo stood silent briefly, not knowing what to say. He wanted to say that he cared about the people of Angustias and would find it difficult to sleep unless he had a more definite idea where the black Jeep was parked. This would sound like an accusation against the mayor, and it was, but he knew that throwing out accusations wouldn't be helpful at the moment.

"Are you going home, too?" he asked the deputy mayor.

Miguel Belen shrugged. "I'll stay a little longer," he said. "Then I'll go out and see how the detectives are doing before heading home."

The sheriff looked around the office so as not to make his departure seem too abrupt, though he didn't really think his mayor cared so long as he left. He remembered the shotgun he had given Primavera earlier.

"Bring out the shotgun, and I'll store it in the gun cabinet at the station house."

Primavera looked at his deputy, but Belen had no suggestions.

"We can't give you the gun . . ." Primavera sputtered.

"What do you mean?"

"I mean . . . The shotgun is . . ."

"The criminal has come into this office before, Gonzalo. He might try to come after us," Belen put in. "And you can't protect us. I have the shotgun in my car and the mayor is going to take the handgun from the desk with him." Belen looked at the mayor who fished out the gun and put it in his briefcase.

"It won't do you any good in the briefcase," Gonzalo volunteered. "Carry it in your jacket pocket."

Primavera did as he was told.

"Thank you, Gonzalo. Good idea."

Gonzalo noted Primavera's nervousness. He decided to push the gun issue just a bit further. He turned to Belen.

"If you want, I can trade you a handgun for the twelve gauge; it would be easier to handle—"

Belen put up a hand to stop him. "The shotgun will do fine," he said. "I've used them before."

Gonzalo dropped the issue. The men he considered his superiors didn't feel like talking, and neither did he. If they wanted to go home, it left the field open for him to conduct the investigation as he saw fit.

His next stop was a brief discussion with Maria Garcia. The lights were on in her home, and Gonzalo cut diagonally across the plaza to knock on her door. She opened, her reading glasses on and a sheath of papers in one hand. He spoke to her at the doorway.

"Anything on the Ortiz children?" he asked.

She answered in spitfire fashion. "Oh, yeah. It was simple. Pedro owned the property free and clear. The children are the heirs. They do have a set of grandparents. They live in Comerio; you probably know them, they moved out of Angustias a few years ago. I already had Child Services place the boy with them. They're old, but they can take care of him. I started the paperwork on a trust fund." She smiled at the end of this litany of activity.

"You said I might know the grandparents," Gonzalo pointed out.

"Oh, yes. Let me see, Hernando and Perfecta Perez Vega."

"I remember them, Esmeralda's parents. They moved out more

than a few years ago, maybe twenty years ago. Anyway, do you have a phone number for them?"

Maria Garcia went into the room she kept as a home office and came back less than a minute later with a phone number on a scrap of paper.

"Remember, Gonzalo," she said, handing him the number. "I think of them as my clients, so don't badger, bully, or otherwise molest them. They're in mourning."

"I just need to know if they have any idea who might have done something like this, did Pedro speak of anyone giving him trouble, things like that."

"I met with them; they were shocked at the news."

It was clear that Maria Garcia was going into a defensive mode, so Gonzalo thanked her for the number and told her not to worry. She watched him from her doorway as he crossed the plaza and rounded the corner.

At the door of his office, Gonzalo debated whether to call the grandparents or drive over. He looked at his watch; it was four-thirty and he had promised Mari that he would come home to eat. He went in. A phone call was impersonal and cold at a time like this, but, he rationalized, maybe that was better than a more emotional face-to-face meeting. He made the call.

Mr. Perez picked up the phone. Gonzalo offered Esmeralda's father his condolences but was distracted by Hernandito crying in the background.

"Is he hungry?" Gonzalo asked.

"Huh?"

"Is the boy hungry?"

"We fed him a few minutes ago. I don't know what's wrong with him."

"Maybe it's gas," Gonzalo suggested.

"We burped him," Hernando replied.

"Sometimes it takes more than one burping."

"Look, do you want to come over here and help us out, Sheriff? Or do you have some other reason for calling? Did you catch whoever killed Pedro?"

"We got one of them. He's dead now. The other is still on the loose. I was wondering if you might be able to tell me anything about any problems Pedro was involved in."

"Like what?"

"I don't know. Maybe debts. Maybe someone was giving him trouble. Anything."

Mr. Perez thought about this for half a minute. Hernandito quieted in the background.

"He had a little trouble in the spring," Mr. Perez offered.

"What happened in the spring?"

"He lost two workers right as he was trying to plant a field of *platanos* and *yautia*. He had to give up on it."

"Did he have arguments with them? Violence?"

"No, no. He said they just left. Didn't want to work. He had cleared away a piece of land, maybe an acre, but he hadn't bought the little seedlings. He was frustrated, but not out any real money."

"Do you know the names of these workers?" Gonzalo asked.

"No. It was a minor thing; he just mentioned it in passing, but you said 'anything' so I thought I should say it."

"Thank you very much," Gonzalo said, then he gave Mr. Perez the station house phone number and asked him to leave a message on the answering machine if he thought of anything else that might help explain why the family had been attacked.

Gonzalo had called with the hope that Mr. Perez might know the whereabouts of the missing money, but it seemed clear that Mr. Perez knew nothing about it. Still, the disgruntled workers provided Gonzalo with another angle to work. He tried to think through the possibility that one of these men might have taken the money. They knew the land; they might have stumbled across the money while working on the farm. He didn't see any hitches in this line of thought.

Gonzalo's next stop was the Ortiz home. The road over was in the shadow of tall trees so that even though the sun had a few hours before being officially down, he put on the squad car's headlights. When he got there, he illuminated the detectives talking with Hector on the Ortiz lawn.

"What do you have?" he asked.

Detective Montalvo made his report. They had retrieved four bullet casings that had been drained through a hole in the floor. Other than that, there wasn't much new to the case.

"Four? I only saw two head wounds," Gonzalo said.

"Yeah. We're thinking that maybe they fired off a couple of rounds to show the gun was real and scare the victims."

"That doesn't make too much sense. The way we see it, Pedro already had two bullets in him. What more proof could anyone want? I can't imagine Esmeralda wasn't scared as soon as she caught sight of these guys."

"Okay, then, put it down to a struggle. The wife could have lunged for the gun, a shot or two went off accidentally in the fight."

Gonzalo wasn't much more satisfied with this explanation, but he let it go.

"We called the medical examiner to pick up the bodies. Did you get anything?" Montalvo asked.

"Nope. The Ortiz girl is in a coma; the son is all right. His grandparents have him. That's really about it."

"What are their names?" Detective Rivera asked.

"I've spoken with them already. Not useful."

"But maybe we have better questions to ask. Maybe they'll open up to us," Rivera said. He was pulling out a notepad and pen.

"I'd rather that you guys didn't disturb them. They did just lose a child. You know how it is." Gonzalo was hoping that this aspect of the conversation would end there.

"Well, we still need the names for our records. This is an investigation." Rivera tapped his notepad with the point of his pen. Montalvo gave him a glance that told him not to push, but maybe because the sunlight was getting dim, the glance went unnoticed.

"Look, they have a lawyer. She lives on the plaza. Talk to her. She has their names, addresses, everything. If this is going to be part of the official record, then I don't want to give you any information that may not be one hundred percent accurate. Her name is Maria Garcia. Her address is Number Twelve on the plaza. It's the only house in good shape there, so it shouldn't be hard to find."

Gonzalo put his hands to his hips and his tone showed that he wasn't in the mood to be pushed around by a fellow law officer. Rivera gave his notepad a final tap with the pen, and then he put it away.

"We'll go visit Garcia," Montalvo said. "Besides, we have to report to the mayor, Primavera, so we'll go to the *alcaldia* at the same time."

"Primavera went home," Gonzalo said.

"Home? Doesn't he realize there's a guy with a gun running around killing his citizens?" Montalvo answered. Gonzalo shrugged.

The detectives drove away, leaving Hector and the sheriff on the lawn. When the car was out of hearing range, Gonzalo spoke.

"Did I ever tell you my theory on the human race, Hector?" he asked.

"No. What is it?"

"It's my theory that the human race is a nasty thing. Of all the people with major roles to play in this case, the only ones I can trust are my own deputies, the Ortiz children, and the dead."

Hector nodded in agreement, but inwardly he was dismayed by a pessimism that rarely engulfed his boss so completely.

"What does the guy in the Jeep want?" Gonzalo asked.

"Money."

"That's right. The killer wants the money. The detectives want Esmeralda's family's address because they're following the money, too; that's the only reason to be so adamant about something I told them was a dead end. You want to know something else?"

"What?"

"If Primavera and Belen are actually in their homes, I will be the most surprised man on this entire island—maybe in the whole Western Hemisphere."

"They're out chasing the money, too?" Hector asked.

"Yup. And one more thing. I think I know who can tell us where the money is. I'm going to go test that theory in a little bit, but what I don't know is where Ramos and Jimenez are."

"I sent them to get something to eat. They should be back soon, I told them to get it to go from Cafetín Lolita."

"Well, when they come back, take Jimenez with you and get yourself something to eat, too. This is going to be a long night. It's past five o'clock and I have a date with Mari from six to seven, and I am not going to give up that hour for anything in the world."

Gonzalo started to walk to his car, but turned back.

"You should know, Hector, that I was looking into any possible connection the mayor might have with this drug problem. I don't have anything definite, just a hunch that hasn't gone anywhere yet. I only made one mistake when I started checking the mayor's background."

"What's that?" Hector asked. His eyes had widened at the news that the mayor was under investigation.

"I didn't ask any questions about the deputy mayor, Belen. The more I see of him, the more I see a snake in the grass today."

"Don't quote me on that," Gonzalo tossed over his shoulder as he went back to his car. "And don't share this with anyone."

Hector waved to his boss as the car pulled away and headed back, once again, to the center of town.

CHAPTER FIFTEEN

Gonzalo had referred the detectives to Maria Garcia because he knew there was no chance they would get information from her. He had known and worked with her for years, and she still didn't trust him when it came to those she considered her clients. She was much less likely to trust officers she had never met before.

Detective Montalvo understood this as well.

"Why'd you have to push him?" he asked on the ride over.

Rivera shot him a glance.

"What's the big deal? We're moving a step closer, aren't we?"

"We'll see about that. This Maria Garcia has no incentive to talk to us, if the sheriff isn't going to share info. We're fishing, and she's going to know it as soon as we open our mouths, if she has half a brain."

"Maybe she doesn't. Anyway, the job is to get the money and get control of the situation. It's a good bet Esmeralda's father has the money . . ."

Montalvo raised his hand as though he were going to reach across and slap his partner, but he refrained.

"First off, now Gonzalo knows we're here for the money. Secondly, I don't think Pedro would have held out while his wife and daughter were shot in the head if he knew his father-in-law had the money and could deliver it whenever he wanted. Anyway, we're here. We'll try it your way. Let's go talk to the lawyer lady."

Montalvo was right about not getting information from Maria Garcia. She opened the door, looked both detectives up and down, and made up her mind before saying hello that she was not going to give them any more than could be found on her business card. She started with an aggressive tone.

"Let me guess. You guys are looking for a large sum of money; Gonzalo told you I found some relatives and you want to talk to them. I'll tell you they don't have the money, but you won't care anyway. You want to check for yourselves. Fine. But if Gonzalo didn't give you their name and address, what makes you think I'm going to? If you have any real questions, I'll ask them. If not, leave them alone—they're not witnesses, they're not criminals, they are collateral damage."

She stood in the doorway, giving them a few seconds to come up with a reply. Detective Rivera opened his mouth briefly, then shut it.

"If there's nothing else," Maria continued, "then I will wish you both a pleasant evening. I suggest getting something to eat soon—Cafetín Lolita is the only decent place to eat around here and she'll close up early if there's no business." She peered at their nameplates. "Sergeant Rivera, Captain Montalvo, good night." And she closed the door.

Montalvo turned to his partner. He was clearly not happy. "See?" was all he said.

The detectives turned away slowly, half feeling that they should try again and harder, but that would only draw attention to themselves. They headed for the *alcaldia*. The door was open but there was only minimal hallway lighting. The mayor's office door was locked, as was the door to Miguel Belen's office.

Rivera looked to his superior.

"You don't trust these guys?"

"I trust Primavera less than I trust Belen, and I don't trust Belen at all," Montalvo answered.

He pulled a small set of lock picks from a leather pocket on his gun belt. The mayor's door was open in less than half a minute. Rivera was about to step in, but his partner stopped, grabbing his upper arm.

"I just thought of something," Montalvo said. "The place might be alarmed."

"Angustias? Why? Nothing ever happens here," was Rivera's answer.

"Nothing, huh? What about two years ago? You never worked with Nestor Ochoa, but believe me, he made things happen here then," Montalvo said.

"Okay, we picked the lock already. If it's alarmed we just say the door was unlocked and we were looking for the mayor."

Rivera's solution was good enough for Montalvo and the two men went in. They used their flashlights to search the drawers, a liquor cabinet, and behind the two paintings. They tried sliding their feet over each of the floor tiles to see if any of them moved, but each was solid and appeared untouched. If the money was in the office, both men decided that it was too well hidden to find without a crowbar and more time than they could safely take. They also decided that there was no alarm system, silent or otherwise.

On their way out of the office, Montalvo smiled. There was a three-foot-tall vase near the door that was sometimes used as an umbrella stand. He walked over and shone a light in and walked away, his face turned to disappointment.

They went through the same process in Belen's office with the same results. Wherever the money was, it wasn't going to be easy to get. They made sure the doors were locked as they left, and walked to the station house. Once inside, Montalvo picked the lock on Gonzalo's desk and took a look into the deep side drawers. These revealed a small pile of books in one and hanging files in the other. Though a half million dollars could never be hidden in the lap drawer of the desk, Montalvo searched this too and found Gonzalo's notes concerning Primavera's political connections. He held them up for his partner to read.

"See?" he asked. "He's already looking in the right direction. He's been following up on Primavera. Let's see, he's checked off four names. When he gets a chance, he'll follow up on leads. He'll get the right people."

"Destroy the paper," Rivera said.

"What for? He's already made the calls. Even if I destroy the paper, it's only four names. It won't be that hard to remember. Wherever he got these names from is a source that's still out there. If he digs, he'll get more names. This isn't going to explode. It already exploded." Montalvo shook the paper in his partner's face for emphasis and the station house door opened.

Lucy Aponte put her head in. "Knock, knock," she said.

Lucy was young and pretty with short dark hair that she tucked behind her ears. She was petite with a large smile, pert nose, and bright brown eyes. Cute. Detective Rivera was smitten with his first look, and she knew it.

"Can we help you?" Montalvo asked. He sounded a bit gruff and had instantly decided not to try to hide the papers in his hand or to close the drawer.

"Hi, I was wondering if I could use the phone. My phone is down." She spoke to Rivera.

"There's a pay phone near the plaza," Montalvo answered.

"Then do you have change?" She pulled out a twenty-dollar bill. Rivera started to fish in his pockets. Montalvo sighed and motioned at the phone on Gonzalo's desk.

"Make it quick," he ordered.

She picked up the receiver and dialed an impossibly long number.

"Lady," Montalvo said. "Who the hell are you calling?"

"Oh, a friend. She's in Mexico . . ."

"Get out," Montalvo barked and pointed to the door.

Lucy hung up and pouted at Rivera. He pouted back and walked her to the door.

"Do you live near here?" he asked, opening the door for her to leave.

"Sure, right on the plaza. Number Forty-two."

"Would you like me to escort you home?" Rivera asked.

"Don't you have work to do?" Lucy asked, speaking her best flirt.

"Yeah," Montalvo piped in from his seat at the desk. "Don't you?"

It was Rivera's turn to pout. Lucy reached up and pinched his cheek.

"Maybe we'll meet later?" Rivera was hopeful.

"Maybe. I'll just make my call from a girlfriend's house."

Lucy walked away, and Rivera watched. She turned the corner, looked behind her, catching Rivera's eye, and waved. He waved back and closed the door. A few seconds later, he heard the peel of tires and opened the door again just in time to see Lucy driving off in a red Porsche convertible.

"She drives a Porsche," Rivera told his partner. He was almost giddy. "Man, a hot chick in a Porsche. Number Forty-two, I will see you tonight," he said to himself since Montalvo wasn't listening. Instead he was putting the papers back into the drawer and locking it.

"I hate to break it to you, Romeo, but I don't think there is a Number Forty-two on the plaza," Montalvo said, and it was clear that he didn't really hate breaking the news.

"What do you mean?"

"I mean the lawyer lady's house was Number Twelve. There were four more houses on that side; I assume they're Fourteen, Sixteen, Eighteen, and Twenty. That's it. No Number Forty-two."

"Maybe I misheard her," Rivera said. He was rubbing his forehead, trying to coax a number that would work from what his memory told him of the conversation. Montalvo rolled his eyes.

"Maybe you did. Can we possibly go see Primavera and keep ourselves focused on getting the money? If Gonzalo finds it, nobody is going to be happy."

"What about the list?" Rivera asked.

"Who knows? Maybe Gonzalo will have an accident tonight and we don't have to worry about anything."

The men left the station house, got into their squad car, and drove away.

Meanwhile, Lucy Aponte's heart was racing, and the engine on her leased Porsche was keeping pace. She headed for the Ortiz home, hoping to find Gonzalo. When she pulled up in front, Officer Jimenez was sitting in his squad car, his head tilted back and his arm dangling out of the window as though he was asleep or dead. He sat up straight when Lucy came to a stop.

"Where's Gonzalo?" she asked from her car.

"He left a little while ago to go eat. His mother's house, I think." Jimenez said this and it was only after Lucy pulled back onto the road that he wondered whether he should have given out Gonzalo's location to a woman he didn't know. "Anyway, he's got a gun," he told himself and tilted his head back again.

Like most who spent time in Angustias, Lucy knew Gonzalo's mother lived a hundred yards or so down the road from her sheriff son. In any event, Lucy knew where Gonzalo lived and figured she would stop in at whichever house had a squad car parked in front. The strategy worked. Gonzalo had gotten to his mother's house only a few minutes before. She pulled an envelope out of her glove compartment and let her herself in through the ironwork gate that opened onto the front porch. The front door was open, but she knocked at the screen door. She heard the noise of a chair being pushed back from the dinner table, and Gonzalo himself came to the door, turning on the porch light as he did.

"Aponte? Come in."

"No, no. You come out." She waggled the envelope in front of her.

"What's this about?" Gonzalo asked, stepping out onto the porch.

"I went to the station house to find you, but guess what I found instead."

Gonzalo shrugged. His dinner was on the table, and he sorely wanted to get to it.

"This Captain Montalvo was rifling through your desk drawers."

"I left my desk locked," Gonzalo said as though to prove that she must have been mistaken. He realized his error as the words were coming off his lips.

"I watched those two, the captain and the sergeant. They talked to Maria Garcia for about a minute, then they searched the government building with flashlights, then they went into the station house . . ."

"What exactly are you doing snooping around after the detectives?"

"I wasn't planning to. I was going to go straight to the station house, but I saw Montalvo. Remember Nestor Ochoa? Remember Rincón?" she asked.

Of course he remembered Rincón. The incidents on the beach of Rincón where a boatload of illegal immigrants from the Dominican Republic had crashed, killing dozens, had been the spark that a few days later raged into the worst day in Gonzalo's memory.

"Montalvo was there," Lucy continued. "I took his photo. He was a lieutenant then, but it's him. He's the one who tried to get my film the next day. He's as dirty as they come. When I saw him in town, I had to follow."

"And you confronted him?" Gonzalo asked.

"I pretended I needed the phone. He didn't recognize me."

"How sure are you of that?"

"Positive."

"And he was at Rincón?"

"Positive."

Gonzalo thought for a moment.

"Was he in charge?"

"Ochoa ran things. I got the impression Montalvo was there to make sure things went smoothly. I guess if there had been a problem, he would have taken over."

Gonzalo motioned with his chin, pointing out the envelope still in Lucy's hand.

"Is that for me?" he asked.

She handed it to him. "I took some photos at the crime scene. I wanted to give you a duplicate in case mine were better than the ones you have."

"I assume you've sold the story already," Gonzalo said.

Lucy smiled. "Sold and resold. Picked up a pretty penny. This place is becoming a little hornets' nest. First Ochoa, now Montalvo. A few more incidents like this, and I'll be rich."

"Don't joke, Aponte. When Ochoa came to town, people died."

"I know, Gonzalo. I was almost one of them, remember?"

"Well, stay out of Montalvo's way. I don't need him trying to finish what Ochoa started."

"Don't worry about me. I'm a big girl," she answered, starting back to her car. "Besides, the young detective would protect me; he's in love." She shook her butt as she got into the car and made the sheriff smile. He wouldn't deny that she was cute though he had his doubts about Rivera's feelings for her.

She drove off and Gonzalo went in to finish his dinner and watch the last few minutes of the news.

CHAPTER SIXTEEN

If you're hungry at night in Angustias, there are only a very few places to go. Cafetín Lolita is on a side street coming off the central plaza less than two hundred yards from the station house. Lolita, the owner, serves soup when it isn't too hot, seafood when she's in the mood for it, and rice, beans, plantains, chicken, and pork every day except those days she decides not to open at all. She also makes special dishes from local fruits and vegetables like *malanga, yautia,* and *pana.* The food is good.

Fidel Castro was hungry at six P.M. but he did not want to travel into the center of town. He opted instead to enter Colmado Ruiz, a store on a crossroads near the limits of Angustias. The store was squat and wide, something like its owner, and it served several purposes—there were two pool tables in the front along with two sets of tables and chairs and refrigerators with milk, soda, and beer. A refrigerated display case held cold cut meats waiting to be sliced, and another display case stocked roasted chickens under lights. There were four rows of shelves with canned and boxed goods, and a row of bottles behind the counter from which Ruiz served rum and other hard liquors into disposable plastic cups, fifty cents for every alcoholic inch. A microwave oven and a nineteen-inch television rounded out the store's furnishings.

Castro parked his Jeep to the left of the store where Ruiz received deliveries. He tried the side door, but it was locked. He wasn't the first person in the history of Colmado Ruiz to try to filch merchandise this way, and for many years there had been a padlock on the inside of this door.

Before heading around to the front door of the store, Castro stepped back to the Jeep. He would have been satisfied with a couple of candy bars though he really wanted something hot. He had eaten breakfast early and spent the hours since killing the Ortiz family driving throughout Angustias and the surrounding towns hunting people down who had been named to him in a quick phone call—small-time criminals in the area. Then, when the list had been exhausted, making another call and getting another list. It was hard work finding these men, forcing them to their knees or into a corner, punishing them with a kick or a punch when they lied to him, putting a gun to their foreheads or in their mouths until they cried and yelled "I don't know anything about it" and he was convinced they were telling the truth. Once Daniel was injured, he had had to do all this by himself. Several men had struggled to get away from him or to take his shotgun; he had gotten four elbows in the face so far, and he wasn't done with his second list yet. He couldn't work on an empty stomach. He took the shotgun and walked in the front door with it dangling at his side.

The two men playing pool and the one man drinking a bottled

beer at one of the tables while watching a Yankee game all stopped in midmotion when they saw the young man with the gun. Rafael Ruiz was behind the counter, his back turned to the entrance. He was dusting the bottles on the shelf. He saw Castro coming toward him in the plate glass mirror. This wasn't the first time a gun-toting youth had entered the store. Ruiz had a stump where his left hand used to be due to a young man like Castro with a shotgun like the one Castro carried. Ruiz had a stump, and now he had a handgun, a .357 magnum. He'd have to turn around and reach under the counter to get it, but it was there.

Castro lifted the shotgun above the counter, and Ruiz turned slowly, his hand and his stump up.

"*¡Dame un cubano!*" Castro yelled. "Give me a Cuban sandwich."

"You can put down the gun," Ruiz said in his calmest, most even tone.

Castro pressed the shotgun barrel hard into Ruiz's chest, showing how little inclined he was to resting the weapon in any less-threatening position. Ruiz shrugged, indicating how sorry he was his customer could not be more amenable. He went about making the sandwich, holding the roll down with his stump while slicing it open, filling it with pork and cheeses, putting it, open, into the microwave set for two minutes.

"Give me a Coke and rum," Castro said during the wait. Apparently, the sight of food being prepared had calmed him a little, while building his thirst.

Ruiz turned again to his shelf of liquors and selected a Bacardi; he pulled out a plastic cup and started to pour.

"I want the whole bottle. The whole bottle of rum and the whole bottle of Coke," Castro explained, his irritability rising.

"I don't have a glass that big," Ruiz answered. He also was becoming annoyed.

"Don't mix them; just open the bottles."

"The cold Cokes are in the refrigerator in the back," Ruiz said.

"Well, go get one."

Ruiz did as he was told, then served the sandwich on a Styrofoam plate with a paper napkin. Castro took the sandwich one-handed, and meat fell onto the counter.

"Why don't you put the gun down to eat?" Ruiz asked; he came close to offering to hold the weapon.

Castro swallowed hard, took a chug from the Coke bottle, and answered.

"I'm not some disgusting freak," he said, using his chin to point out Ruiz's stump. "I have two hands."

For Ruiz, the insult was deeply felt. He wasn't normally an emotional man, but the loss of his hand was the most traumatic experience of his life. The man who had shot him did it for sadistic pleasure. He had come in with friends, also armed, and there had been nothing for Ruiz to do but put his hand on the counter as ordered and watch as the man put the shotgun muzzle to his wrist and pulled the trigger. Castro's joke left Ruiz trembling with anger. Castro took the trembling for a sign of weakness and smiled.

In his hungry attack on the sandwich, Castro lost track of the man who had been watching baseball. That man left the store quietly and ran once he got outside. The pool players were not as lucky; they stood in the gunman's peripheral vision, watching the scene between Castro and Ruiz, glad not to attract attention. Castro's burning hunger pains began to be replaced by the sharper pain of swallowing food unchewed and gulping Coke. He couldn't stop himself or slow down, his hunger had been so intense. He wasn't the only hungry person in Angustias, however.

After driving to the Cafetín Lolita where Ramos and Jimenez

had eaten to satisfaction, and finding it now closed, Hector had Ramos drive him out to the Colmado Ruiz. Hector's hunger was as profound as Castro's. His hands were developing a slight trembling. The squad car pulled up on the right side of the store where a side door, unlike the one on the left, was thrown wide open to receive whatever breezes the July night air might bring. Ramos did not, however, pull up even with the door, so the scene between Castro and Ruiz remained hidden from the officers. Castro also saw nothing. Only Ruiz saw anything useful—the front of the police vehicle. He looked away from the side door, not wanting to telegraph the arrival of his saviors.

Castro looked to where Ruiz looked, following his line of sight to the pool players; these men looked away, not happy to have attracted his attention. Then Officer Ramos was heard saying something at the side door. He was talking over his shoulder to Hector as he stepped into the store. Castro wheeled about and fired, hitting Ramos square in the chest, knocking him hard onto his back, his scalp opening on the asphalt, the shot leaving him nearly unconscious.

Ruiz took this second and a half of distraction as an opportunity to grab not the .357 under the counter but Castro's rum bottle. Ruiz was a short man so even though he almost left his feet stretching across the counter, he failed to reach the back of Castro's head. Instead, he hit him high between the shoulder blades. This hurt, but it wasn't near to being incapacitating. Castro ducked as though he thought the ceiling was falling on him. He pumped another shell, turned, and fired, but Ruiz had already thrown himself back behind the counter, lost his balance, and fallen to the floor. The shot exploded several liquor bottles and shattered the mirror. Glass rained on the store owner with a mix of the finest rums of Puerto Rico. When Castro turned back to the side door, he found Hector in the store, his side arm in both hands and aimed for Castro's heart. Castro fired without aiming, but one pellet found Hector's right hand and scratched it. His gun clattered to the floor as Castro chambered another shell.

In the fraction of a second it took to pump the shotgun, Hector leaped to within a yard of the shooter and squatted as another round was fired over his head. He reached for his nightstick and came out of the crouch swinging. He missed Castro, who had leaned back to avoid the swing. Castro overcompensated in trying to regain his balance and lurched forward again, stepping into Hector's two-handed second swing. The sound, the pool players said later, was like one of those fake home-run sounds from the old-time newsreels. Castro dropped his weapon and fell to his knees. Hector sprang on him, knocked him to the ground, and cuffed his hands behind his back before checking on his partner.

Gonzalo finished his dinner, his nine-year-old Sonia sitting on the sofa by his side, his elbows resting on his knees. They watched the last few minutes of the evening news. The anchor recapped the day's events, mentioning the fire and murders in Angustias briefly, showing a still photo that Gonzalo knew had come from Lucy Aponte. The top story of the day, however, was the protest of students and union workers. Gonzalo laughed out loud watching the coverage of a hyped rally that had spent all day fizzling. Captain Montalvo was in charge of a squad of officers protecting the governor's mansion in San Juan, La Fortaleza. The protestors were expected to head that way, but they never showed up. Montalvo gave a seven-second sound bite, saying it was better to be safe than sorry—in that sense the huge police detail did exactly what it was supposed to. As he carried his plate to the kitchen, Gonzalo tried to figure out whether Montalvo had forgotten about the sound bite when he said he'd spent the day booking disorderlies or if he didn't care if the sheriff of Angustias caught him in a lie.

"Do you want more?" Mari asked.

"Nope. I piled on the seconds the first time around," he told her.

"Are you going to be going back out now?"

Gonzalo looked at his watch, which read exactly six-thirty, and then looked at his daughter.

"I told myself I would rest for an hour. I've got thirty minutes left," he said.

"Those detectives from San Juan have everything under control?" Mari asked.

"Yup. They have everything under control for the next thirty minutes at least."

Gonzalo sat with his wife and child, and his mother sat in her favorite chair and took up some crochet work. They watched a show made up of comedic skits. At the first commercial break, Gonzalo's mother spoke.

"Collazo killed the guy who killed the Ortiz family?" she asked. He noticed that she had lost most of the slurring that her stroke had left her with.

"He got one of them."

"How many more are there?"

"A few," Gonzalo said. "But don't worry. Not many of them are in Angustias, and the ones that are here won't stay for long."

"Where are they going?"

"To jail."

The show came back on and stifled any further conversation. At the next commercial break, Gonzalo got up. He had taken time for a quick shower before dinner and was dressed in a completely smoke- and soot-free uniform for the first time in many hours. He put on his shoes now. He still had eight minutes remaining of the hour he had promised himself and his family. He sat next to Mari again with his gun belt in hand. A minute later and seven minutes before the end of his free time, his radio came to life. It was Hector.

"Sorry to bother you, chief, but I've got a good-news, bad-news situation." The message was coming through poorly.

"Explain," Gonzalo said, getting up and leaving the room.

"We have Castro in custody. Ramos is injured."

"How bad?" Gonzalo asked.

The response was unclear, but Gonzalo made out the word "concussion."

"Where are you?" Gonzalo asked.

"Clinica Mendoza."

"Castro?"

"Same."

Gonzalo looked at his watch. "Any emergency?"

"No. Montalvo and Rivera . . ."

Gonzalo couldn't get the rest. Though not very far away, the clinic was in a different valley from the one his mother lived in.

"I'll be there in a few minutes," Gonzalo said, but there was no response from Hector, so he wasn't sure the message was heard.

When he went back into the living room, he stood behind the sofa watching the last half of a skit that would have made much more sense if he had seen its first half. When the skit finished, it was seven, and his time was up. He bent over to kiss Mari on the top of her head.

"What time do we leave tomorrow?" he asked.

Mari sighed. She knew he was going to try to leave as late as possible, forcing a rush through the airport. She hated cutting things so close.

"The plane leaves at eight-forty in the evening. We're supposed to be there at least ninety minutes before. It takes about forty-five minutes to get to the airport, an hour to be safe. You do the math," she said.

Gonzalo rolled his eyes up, searching his brain for the correct calculation. "We have to leave around six?" he asked.

"That's what we discussed a dozen times before," his wife said.

"Piece of cake."

He stooped to kiss his daughter's hair, gave his mother a quick hug, and went out to his car.

CHAPTER SEVENTEEN

Gonzalo didn't rush on his way to the clinic. Fidel Castro was a dangerous man and a killer, so it was good to get him off the streets, but Castro alone was not the reason the Ortiz family was murdered. He pulled the trigger, but someone else gave the order. Castro wasn't a drug kingpin. If he was killing people and running around looking for a bagful of money, it wasn't out of possessiveness; it was out of fear. Like Maria Garcia pointed out, drug lords have others to do their dirty work; Castro was one of those others. More than anything during the drive to the clinic, Gonzalo wanted to know who Castro was working for.

The one part of police work Gonzalo prided himself on was his interrogation technique. His specialty was setting up a series of questions that exposed the suspect's fears. What suspects feared most was usually the truth—they might not confess, but knowing the truth helped narrow the field of investigation; it directed the examination of evidence. Getting these results, however, required forethought. You couldn't just go into an interview and say "Where's the body?" Or, in this case, "Who sent you?" In some ways, the interrogation was like a play with a script of questions, props like the tape recorder, pens, pads of paper, a clipboard, and dramatic effects to be staged, like interruptions from outside, urgent phone calls, that gave suspects time to think or threatened to take that time away.

Gonzalo thought of his lines as he swung his car into the clinic parking lot, passing Dr. Perez's sky blue VW bug as it went out. There were only six or seven other cars in the lot, including Hector's squad car. The clinic had gotten along for years with one doctor, one nurse, two exam rooms, and parking space for about five. A few years earlier, Martin Mendoza had been plagued with a tax problem so complicated even he couldn't explain it. He would shrug his shoulders and say, "It's one of those things," when asked about it. The settlement resulted in millions for the clinic—more doctors, nurses, and many, many more parking spaces. The few cars that were in the lot only deepened its profound look of desolation. Gonzalo parked near the clinic and was thinking of a set of questions to ask Castro as he entered the clinic. The first person he met was Hector.

"How's Ramos?" he asked.

"He's all right. In and out. Broke two ribs and one head," Hector said. He pointed to his own head. "He'll be in plenty of pain tomorrow."

"And Iris?"

"Drugged up a little, but lucid enough."

"You spoke with her? Good. Partners support each other," Gonzalo said. "Even on a crazy day like this. How about our friend, Castro?"

"I cracked him pretty good with the baton." Hector motioned a baseball swing. "His ear is split." He pointed to his own left ear. "His scalp was bleeding; his eye was shut."

"Geez. You sure you hit him once?"

"Just once, boss, but I didn't hold back. Believe me—he wasn't in the mood for more. Maybe a mild concussion, the doctor said."

"Excessive force?" Gonzalo asked. This was not a conviction he could afford to risk amid charges of police brutality.

"He had a shotgun; I had a nightstick."

"Where was your weapon?"

Hector held up his right hand. There was a small patch of gauze taped to the back of his hand.

"He shot me. Two stitches. My gun was on the floor, or I would have been happy to use that instead. It was either smash him or surrender. It didn't look like he was taking prisoners."

"Okay. I'm just asking questions you're going to hear a few more times before the trial. Anyway, where is he now?"

"Rivera's with him in one of the offices. He started the interrogation."

"Rivera?"

"Montalvo's in the bathroom."

"Great," Gonzalo said. He put his hands to his hips and looked to the ground. He decided to step away from the interrogation for now. It would be worse than useless for him to jump into a questioning already in progress. There would be plenty more questions to ask when the detectives were done.

"Can I see Ramos?"

Hector shrugged and pointed at a closed examination-room door.

"Perez is in there with him."

"Perez just drove out," Gonzalo said, thumbing over his shoulder toward the parking lot.

"Nope," Hector answered. "I saw him go in, and I've been standing right here . . ."

Gonzalo was already moving to the exam room Hector had pointed out. He turned the knob and swung the door open. Dr. Perez was explaining something to Officer Ramos, who was semireclined on an exam table, his head and chest bandaged, his eyes glazed with either medication or boredom. Perez turned to Gonzalo with annoyance on his face.

"Can I help—" he started, but Gonzalo let out a "Damn it" under his breath and jogged down the corridor to the offices. Only one of the offices had a closed door. It was heavy and solid to keep the occasional junkie patient from breaking in at night for triplicate prescription pads. It was unlocked at this hour, and Gonzalo swung it open. It scraped the crown of Rivera's head; he was on all fours and alone.

"Damn it," Gonzalo said, leaving Rivera to hold his head with one hand as he used the other to clutch the doorknob and pull himself up. He was bleeding from the mouth and blinking as though trying to correct his vision.

"Where's the shotgun?" Gonzalo asked Hector as he hurried back to the lobby.

"In the trunk."

"Go check, then get on the road. You're looking for Perez's VW."

"Which way did it go?"

Gonzalo pointed in the general direction of the plaza a couple of miles away. Hector ran out to his car knowing that there could be no more definite details. The road between the clinic and the center of town branched off several times and an honest estimate gave Castro a six- or seven-minute lead that could put him out of Angustias altogether.

Montalvo came out of the bathroom, still fastening his gun belt, the sound of the flushing toilet behind him.

"What did I miss?" he asked.

Gonzalo glared at him. He didn't know whether to accuse the *Metropolitanos* of incompetence or of a conspiracy to get Castro back on the streets. It took him a full second to decide to say nothing on either score just yet; instead, he'd keep Montalvo and Rivera out of the loop as far as possible. Even if they weren't dirty, they still weren't very good.

"Castro's back on the loose, in a sky blue VW bug," Gonzalo said.

Montalvo sidled past him into the office with Rivera, who kept touching the top of his head, pulling his hand away with a smear of blood on a fingertip. Gonzalo followed Montalvo to the doorway. Locking both men in the office flashed through Gonzalo's mind—it would allow him some minutes at least to do his job in peace—but he rejected the idea; the door locked from the inside.

Montalvo opened his mouth, and Gonzalo knew it would be to start giving orders and taking control. He beat the detective to the punch.

"You." He pointed at Rivera. "Get your head examined. You'll need a couple of stitches. You." He pointed at Montalvo. "Call the mayor, let him know the situation. Give him the full briefing and ask him what he wants to do next. Then contact your precinct and see if they can't send you a few uniforms. We need to put a lid on this guy."

Gonzalo left the office doorway and Dr. Perez stepped in, taking a look at the top of Rivera's head. He had given Gonzalo a look as he entered that the sheriff interpreted to mean "Please bring my car back safe." The VW was Perez's obsession, washed daily and in perfect running order with well over a hundred thousand hill-country miles on it. Gonzalo paused to get the doctor's plate number and ran to the clinic's entrance to shout it out to Hector, who was just getting into the squad car.

Montalvo stepped out of the office, following after Gonzalo for a step before thinking better of it. He wanted to say he should be in charge of finding Castro, but then he really wanted to speak to the mayor.

"Sheriff," he called out. "The mayor's home number?"

Gonzalo turned to face him but kept moving toward one of the exam rooms. "I don't know it off the top of my head," he said. "He's listed."

Gonzalo ducked his head into the room Iris Calderon occupied. She was slowly getting into her mud-covered uniform trousers. It was clear the stooping and the raising of her head were exacting a toll felt in pain.

"What's the commotion?" she asked.

"I'll tell you in the car," her sheriff said. He wanted to tell her both that she should hurry and that she should take her time. He said nothing and went out. It took a few seconds longer for Calderon to get her pants on. She slipped her feet into her shoes and didn't bother with the laces. Her head was still pounding and breathing caused a dull pain that grew stronger the deeper she inhaled. The drugs she had been given made her care less about her hurt, not hurt less. She walked down the corridor toward the exit slowly, with one hand dragging along the wall.

"Officer Calderon," Montalvo called after her. She stopped but did not turn around for fear that the extra motion would topple her over.

"The mayor's phone number?" he said to her back.

"Look it up," she answered.

"It's not listed," he complained.

"You're the detective," Calderon said, and she continued her walk.

Montalvo tossed his hands in the air and rolled his eyes out of frustration, but he couldn't argue against her point so he let her go without further comment.

The first place Hector stopped in his search for Castro was Colmado Ruiz. He tried telling himself that this would be any good cop's first stop—it was the last place Castro had gone, maybe there was some reason other than the cubano sandwich—but then Hector admitted to himself that a cubano didn't seem like such a bad idea in itself. Of course, if anyone could remember anything about what was said before all the shooting started, that might also be helpful in identifying where Castro might have gone. For instance, if Castro had stood before the counter and stated plainly, "I'm going to eat this sandwich, then I'm going to So-and-so's house."

When Hector got to the store, Ruiz was still cleaning up the glass behind his counter and the pool players were still playing pool. A few neighbors had drifted in after hearing the shots, but drifted back when they saw nothing had happened to the store owner and the action was over. It was no fun watching a one-armed man sweep up shards of glass.

"I have nothing to say," Ruiz said as soon as he saw Hector.

"Okay, how about you wash your hands and make me a cubano?" Hector went to the back and got a soda from the refrigerator. He paid for his food and stood in front of Ruiz to wait for the microwave to do its work.

"Did you see—"

"I saw nothing," Ruiz said.

"Okay, now how about you let me finish the questions before you answer them?" Hector adopted a firm tone; it had been a long day and Ruiz was promising to make it longer than it needed to be.

"Okay. Ask."

"Did you see which direction the guy drove in from?"

"No. I saw him when he was standing behind me. I saw him in the mirror."

"Did he say anything?"

"He asked for the sandwich, he asked for the drinks." Ruiz pulled the hot sandwich from the microwave and handed it to Hector.

"Did he say anything about what he was doing, where he was going, where he had come from? Did he say anything about whether he had to meet someone?"

"Nothing like that. A sandwich, rum, and soda."

Hector took a bite of his sandwich and tried to think of what to ask next.

"Why don't you ask those guys over there?" Ruiz said, pointing at the pool players. "They were here, too."

Hector motioned to the pool players and they put their cues down and stepped over to him.

"Either one of you see where the guy drove in from? Was he coming from up the hill, from down the hill?"

The men Hector spoke with were regulars at the pool table who had never given any trouble, but they looked a bit ragged around the edges. Their clothes were rumpled, their faces unshaven, and they smelled of cigarettes and beer. Hector knew each of them still lived with his parents, and he tried to think whether they were old enough to drink. They were.

"I had my back to the door," one of them said. "I was watching this guy make a shot."

"And I was trying to make the shot. I was concentrating: bank shot, using a bridge."

"Did you make it?"

"Yeah. Hey, why don't you ask the other guy who was here? He was watching the Yankees on TV."

"Who was this?"

"Carlos Velez. He was celebrating. He said Gonzalo let him out of jail."

"Yeah," Hector said. "We're expecting a crowd. I didn't see Carlos here."

"That bastard snuck out," Ruiz threw in. Having acquitted himself well in the fight with Castro, Ruiz had no mercy for someone who chose to "fight another day."

"Where was he when Castro came in?"

"That's the guy's name? Castro?" one of the pool players asked. "What kind of parents would call him that?"

"It's his last name," Hector explained.

"What's his first name? Fidel?"

Hector said nothing, and the pool players laughed when they had drawn their own conclusions.

"You gotta give him a break, man. With a name like that, what else could he do but turn to a life of crime?"

"Very funny. Anyway, did you guys hear him say anything about where he was going, where he had come from?"

"Nothing like that, just 'Give me a sandwich, give me a soda, give me rum.' Very bossy. Like a dictator." The young man who spoke laughed at his own joke, and Hector knew there was no use in asking more questions.

Hector finished his sandwich and took his soda with him to the car. He had the name of another witness and a full stomach, two things he didn't have when he went into the store. Velez lived only a quarter mile away from the store so Hector headed there.

Velez's home was tiny and made of unpainted cinder block. He was allowed to live in it by a brother who had inherited a real house and some land farther down the road. The lights were on until Hector parked in front. He got out and banged on the door.

"I know you're in there, Carlos," Hector yelled through the door. "I saw the lights on; I saw them go off. Open the door."

"I didn't do anything wrong."

"Don't make me knock the door down," Hector said.

Carlos opened the door and Hector pulled him out by his shirt.

"I bet Gonzalo said to go straight home and stay there, right?" Hector asked. "Then why were you in Colmado Ruiz?"

"He didn't say starve," Carlos answered.

"Okay, fair enough. Now did you see the Jeep when the guy pulled into the parking lot?"

"Which Jeep?"

"Don't do that Carlos. Believe me, you'll only be hurting yourself." The look on Hector's face told Carlos that actually, it would be Hector who would be hurting him.

"Okay, okay. The Jeep came driving from up the hill, headed down."

"Like he had just come from town?"

"Well, I don't know where he came from, but that's the right direction, yeah." Carlos crossed his arms and leaned against the wall of his home. In his view, having helped the investigation made him a colleague.

"Okay," Hector said. "Now get back inside and stay there."

"Well, really I gotta—"

"Nothing. If I catch you outside, you're going to be in trouble." Hector wagged his finger at Carlos as he walked back to the squad car. He headed to town to see if the Jeep had been spotted there.

The plaza was quiet except for a couple of young lovers on a bench paying the rest of the world no attention. He went into the station house to check on messages. There were several, some asking what the hell was going on, others wishing Gonzalo a restful vacation. Among the messages, Maria Garcia had more information, Lucy Aponte was taking more photos, and Susana Ortiz, the sheriff of Naranjito, wanted to talk with Gonzalo. "Your little problem," her voice said, "is spilling out into my town."

CHAPTER EIGHTEEN

Francisco Primavera lived alone in a barrio of Angustias called Las Curvas. It was a community set on an undulating road branching off the interstate. Las Curvas was a newly developed area of elaborately designed homes, no two alike, each with some feature to set it apart—one with ramparts, another with a dummy tower, others with arches or round windows. None of the features reflected individual tastes or styles; they were symbols of the lengths the owners would go to to prove they were special people.

The two lawyers Maria Garcia competed against for clients had been among the first to build here; their first wives also had homes in the barrio. Two dentists and two internists who worked in other towns had homes here as well as three or four San Juan businessmen who owned co-ops in the city but could afford estates in Angustias.

Unlike most residents of Las Curvas, and, in fact, unlike most residents of Angustias, Primavera had not built his own home or ordered it built. Instead, he had bought it from a businessman who found he had little time for estates and there was nothing to do in Angustias except admire the view. It was a magnificent view, extending past the hills and valleys all the way to the ocean, but not everyone can enjoy a view.

Primavera's house marked him as the most special person in Las Curvas. The first floor was a pillared parking area and an apartment no one had ever found a use for. The parking was under a balcony accessed by outdoor stairs. The balcony completely surrounded the upper level and each of the four sides had large potted plants and a mix of metal and wicker furnishings—tables with glass tops, rocking chairs, footstools. Round windows, double doors that met in a peaked middle, a walled perennial garden, and a kidney-shaped in-ground pool were some of the amenities and attractions he shared with no one.

Castro's VW exhaust could be heard from a mile away, and when he pulled into the driveway next to three other cars—two belonging to Primavera and the other to Miguel Belen—Primavera and his deputy mayor were both on the balcony above the parking area waiting for him. Belen stood cross-armed and upright with an iced drink in one hand. Primavera leaned with both hands on the iron railing of the balcony. In his right hand, he flicked ashes from a cigar.

Castro got out of the bucket seat of the VW using the door frame to pull himself out. He had a snub-nosed .38 in hand and a bandage showing some blood on his left ear. He took the steps up to the balcony two by two. He stood a half-dozen feet from Primavera and the mayor regarded him as he took a deep drag from the cigar. Belen stood to the right and behind Primavera; he took a sip from his drink.

"How'd you get out?" Primavera asked.

"One of the cops, *Metropolitanos,* the young one. He said I had work to do; he gave me his ankle holster and gun. He said, 'Hit me. Make it good.' I hit him. I made it good. Then I climbed out the window and went to work."

"Did you find the money?" Primavera asked, then put the cigar back in his mouth.

"That wasn't the work I had to do," Castro answered. He raised the gun to Primavera's heart and without styling, without tilting the gun to one side or the other, he pulled the trigger just as the mayor was taking the cigar from his lips in the V of his fingers to say something. Primavera took a half step back, falling as though reluctantly; his cigar hand reached for the railing for support but didn't get any. The cigar rolled off the balcony and onto the parking area below, a soft breeze helping it on its way.

The bullet had crashed through Primavera's sternum, and curved in its trajectory, lodging in a back rib. His left arm flailed for a second as though still looking for the railing, then it stopped. Castro stepped closer and pointed the gun into his face. "No," Belen said, and Castro just stood over his victim, watched him raise his head an inch off the ceramic tiling, cough up a mix of blood and spit, then let his head fall back to the tiles with a dull sound. That was the end of Francisco Primavera, his eyes still open but nothing else about him making any pretense to life.

"You see?" Belen said. "If you had shot him in the head while he was down like that, the coroner would know you shot him without any need—cold-blooded."

"So? I don't even know how many charges they got against me. One more isn't going to make a difference and a shot in the head is as good as one in the chest if he's dead. That detective told me it was the death penalty for me if I was caught. I don't plan on getting caught." Castro turned and was about to go back downstairs to his car.

"You almost done?" Belen asked.

Castro faced him and pulled a slip of paper out of his pant's back pocket.

"I got two more names to check. I talk to them and if I don't get anything, that's it; I leave this dump of a town."

"They're just going to give up on the money?"

Castro shrugged. It wasn't his money. "That's what the *Metropolitanos* told me," he said.

Belen took another sip.

"I gotta go," Castro said. He turned to the stairs again, tucking the gun into his waistband.

"You forgot something," Belen called out.

When Castro turned again, the deputy mayor had a pistol held straight out in front of him in both hands. Castro reached for his own gun just in time to drop it when the first bullet hit him in the gut. The second hit high on his chest. The third one went nowhere near him as he fell backward on the stairs, sliding down several, stopping halfway to the ground floor, his gun clattering two steps farther.

Belen went to the top of the stairs and aimed at Castro. He reminded himself of the warning he had given just a minute earlier. He took his own words seriously; Castro hadn't seen the value of avoiding one in a string of murder charges, but Belen intended to be a hero, not a suspect. He came down the stairs, was uncertain whether Castro was breathing or not, and squatted close to him until he was sure Castro's chest wasn't rising and falling. He pulled the slip of paper from Castro's hand and put it in his own back pocket. He moved on and picked up the handgun by the trigger guard and took it with him to Primavera's kitchen, where he picked up a cordless phone. He dialed the number to the clinic and asked for a doctor, then he called the station house; there was no answer. Then he called the *Metropolitanos* police station in San Juan. When he was done calling and telling his version of the story briefly but often, he pulled up a chair on the balcony and sat watching the dead men with the phone in his lap, Castro's gun on the floor beside his feet, and his own gun still in his hand.

Iris Calderon had been given medications to calm her nerves and ease her pain. She could not have named the meds to save her life, but they had come in the form of a pill in a tiny paper cup and a quick shot into her naked rear end. She had slept for an hour after Dr. Perez finished treating her, and since then she had tried to think of the Ortiz case but she couldn't hold her thoughts together for more than a minute at a time before slipping into memories of her childhood, television shows, natural vistas, geometric shapes that morphed into one another, and, mostly, nothing at all.

Gonzalo had asked her to come along because the VW made a distinct sound and he knew Calderon had studied how radios worked and didn't work in the hills of Angustias. He was hoping knowledge in one area would prove useful in another, but the two studies were not the same. For one thing, radios transmitted specific frequencies and these signals were either received or not by other radios set to pick up exactly the same frequency; rarely was there interference on police channels. The sounds of the VW competed in the valleys with other car sounds, loud televisions or conversations from the houses they passed, and a boom box used by a group of teens sitting and laughing on the metal guardrail that kept cars from going off the road. Making the job more difficult was the relative popularity of the VW bug. It made a distinctive sound, but there were more than a dozen of the cars in Angustias. As soon as Gonzalo explained what he wanted, Calderon told him that the mission was a long shot, but they were already on the road and he wasn't going to turn back.

Two minutes later, they both heard the sound of a Volkswagen.

"Pull over," Calderon ordered.

Gonzalo got onto the shoulder and shut off the engine. The sound was clear but receding; in less than a minute, the sound was lost altogether. There was the sound of owls and *coquis,* a tiny tree frog that serves as the national mascot of Puerto Rico.

"Any ideas?" Gonzalo asked. Calderon turned to her boss and shrugged.

"A guess?"

"If I had to guess, I'd say he just drove past the Ortiz home, headed into town."

"Get on the radio," Gonzalo said. "Get Jimenez."

He started the squad car and pulled back onto the road.

"Jimenez, Jimenez. Do you read me? Jimenez, Jimenez. Do you—"

"I got you loud and clear."

"Did a blue Volky just go by your position?"

"No, ma'am."

"You sure?"

"I'm facing the road. A big white pickup, three guys on horses, two teens on bicycles—that's all the traffic I've had in the past fifteen minutes. No Volkys of any color."

"Okay," Calderon said. And was silent a moment. "Be advised that a sky blue Volky is our Castro's vehicle now. Keep your motor on. If you see him, don't lose sight."

"Is he armed?" Jimenez asked. Calderon looked to the sheriff.

"He shouldn't be," Gonzalo said, but his tone told her that he wouldn't be surprised to find that Castro had sprouted wings and could fly now.

"You should consider him armed and dangerous until you hear otherwise." She gave him the license plate number.

Calderon's next task was to update law enforcement in all the surrounding towns of the situation in a general broadcast. Offers came in from several towns to send squad cars and manpower, and Gonzalo accepted all of them.

With the squad car's engine running and the radio chatter, neither officer heard the shot that killed the mayor of Angustias. They did hear the three shots in quick succession that Miguel Belen fired, but they heard these faintly, and couldn't tell which direction they came from. Gonzalo pulled over and shut down the motor again, in case there were more shots fired, but in half a minute of listening, there was nothing but the night sounds common to Angustias. Gonzalo took the CB into his own hands.

"Did anyone else hear that?" he asked. Jimenez at the Ortiz home and Hector driving up into the sparsely populated barrio of La Cola both reported that they had heard nothing. Gonzalo turned to Calderon.

"What do you think?"

"I think the shots came from behind us," she answered, and Gonzalo made a three-point turn. He drove slowly, trying to cut down the noise from his vehicle in case there were more shots. Two minutes later, the voice of Dr. Perez came over the radio, tentative but clear.

"Hello? Anyone there?"

"Perez. What can we do for you?" Gonzalo answered.

"Hello? Anybody?" Gonzalo heard the doctor again and knew he had not let go of the Speak button. A nurse's voice mumbled something in the background, and the doctor protested that he had depressed the button, then Perez apologized to his audience and said, "Mayor Primavera has been shot. So has the suspect, the young man who was here with the laceration to the ear and scalp. I will be going to Primavera's house with a nurse. Please meet me there." He said all of this with the wooden voice of one reading from a script. Maybe he was, Gonzalo thought.

"Hey, Gonzalo, are you there?" Perez asked. This time he let go of the button.

"I'm here."

"Do you think my car will be there?"

"The sooner you get there, the sooner you'll find out. Just don't pull into Primavera's driveway until I get there."

"Oh, there shouldn't be any danger," the doctor said. "Belen said both men were dead already."

"Then why are you going?"

"I'm not sure. To remove the bodies, I guess."

"Do me a favor, Doctor? Stay where you are. If we need you, I'll call."

The doctor was happy to stay away.

Gonzalo drove the last few hundred yards to Primavera's house quickly and in silence. He pulled up behind the blue VW which, he noted, was in immaculate condition. The doctor would be pleased.

"Stay here," he told Calderon as he got out of the car. She was not keen on climbing stairs anyway, so she just slid down in her seat a bit, making herself comfortable.

On his way up the stairs, Gonzalo stopped to check Castro for a pulse though it was clear there wouldn't be one to find. The young man's mouth, no longer smiling, was opened wide as though waiting for a tongue depressor that couldn't possibly do him any good now. Gonzalo jogged up the rest of the stairs and found Primavera sprawled on his back, the single hole in his chest enough to do the work of killing him, his eyes open and dull, looking at nothing in particular.

Belen was still seated, but he had refilled his glass and lit a cigar, both guns resting on a chair he had pulled up near his. The cigar, the rum on ice, the cool demeanor with two bodies just a few feet away and still warm made Gonzalo think Belen fit the stereotype of evil mastermind just a little too perfectly. He would have liked to see Belen sweat even if only a little.

"Which one did you kill?" the sheriff asked, looking for a rise. Belen smiled instead and took the cigar from his mouth.

"Don't you have a report to file or something?"

"I was asking a serious question," Gonzalo said.

"So was I."

Gonzalo walked over to the chair with the guns. He didn't have latex gloves with him. He stooped to sniff the weapons.

"They've both been fired?" he asked.

Belen took a sip of his drink and pointed to the road leading to Primavera's house.

"It looks like Captain Montalvo is on his way. I'd rather tell the story just once."

"Fine," Gonzalo said, crossing his arms on his chest. "I'll wait."

"No, Gonzalo, you won't. Montalvo will need a detailed report from you and your deputies about the fire this morning, the initial murders, the shooting on the plaza, the shooting of Calderon, the shooting of Ramos. You have a lot of typing to do. Get to work."

"I'm part of this investigation, Belen . . ."

"Not anymore," Belen said. He was still calm, but it wasn't relaxation, it was triumph, like a man who has just declared "Checkmate."

"We asked for homicide detectives, we have homicide detectives, we're going to use homicide detectives. No offense, but you're not a specialist in this area; Montalvo is."

"Montalvo let this Castro guy escape—"

Belen put up his hand to silence the sheriff as Captain Montalvo started to climb the stairs.

"Let's not start comparing records, Gonzalo," Belen said. "Type up your reports, turn over your evidence, get some sleep, and go on your trip tomorrow."

Gonzalo didn't move as Montalvo reached the landing. Belen shooed him with his cigar hand.

"That's an order, Gonzalo."

"An order?"

"Try to remember who is the mayor of Angustias now. That is, if you still want to be sheriff when you get back from wherever it is you're going."

"I work for the Municipal Police of Puerto Rico, not for you, so don't threaten what you can't actually do. I follow orders from mayors who have the best interest of Angustias at heart—the jury's still out on you."

"You think it's an empty threat? Find out tomorrow; for now, just do what I said."

Montalvo stood quietly a few paces behind Gonzalo, studying the tiles, pretending not to hear the drama in front of him. Not wanting to continue the argument in front of the detective, Gonzalo left, passing Rivera going up as he went down the stairs. The detective had a bald spot shaved onto the top of his head with a small patch of gauze looking like an egg in a bird's nest.

"Hey, are you going to help out or what?" Rivera asked.

"I'm going to do my part," Gonzalo answered without turning around.

He went to his squad car, got in, woke up Calderon, and drove away.

"We've got people to talk to," Gonzalo said.

Calderon uh-huhed and closed her eyes again.

CHAPTER NINETEEN

Hector returned Sheriff Ortiz's call himself. His first few years in Angustias, he flirted with Susana Ortiz as often as circumstances allowed. Since crimes brought them together most often, circumstances rarely allowed. It was clear, on occasions that did allow for freer interaction, that he was trying way too hard for a prize he would never get. Susana was simply not interested. She was young and beautiful and driven. Hector, or any other love interest, would have been a distraction from running her station house.

"What kind of trouble are we causing you, Sheriff?" Hector asked.

"Oh, that message is old. Your man in the Jeep was in town, actually in the center of town, shaking down this low-level drug dealer we've had our eye on for a month."

"Shaking down a drug dealer?"

"We have a guy running a camera on this guy. We're trying to collect info on who's buying, who's supplying. We're scheduled to close him down in about another three days. Anyway, your guy comes in, corners this drug dealer, throws a couple of punches into his gut, waves a shotgun, yells at our dealer, and leaves."

"Any idea what he was yelling about?"

"Unfortunately, our guy on the scene could only get a few words on tape: 'Where's the money?' was repeated a few times. The dealer had no idea what he was talking about. He pulled out a wad of cash and tried to give it to the guy, but he slapped it into the gutter."

"He got away."

"Well, you guys caught him, no?"

"He busted out."

The words were followed by silence on both sides of the line.

"Anyone get hurt?" Sheriff Ortiz asked.

"He punched out one of the *Metropolitanos*."

Hector gave as much information about the Volkswagen as he could, but if Castro would attack a drug dealer in the middle of Naranjito in broad daylight, it was clear this operation wasn't so much a search as a chase. He wasn't hiding; he just wasn't staying still long enough to be caught.

"Do you guys need any more help from us?"

"We could use the manpower and a couple more cars if you have them to spare. We're searching everywhere for him."

Two more cars and four more officers were heading to Angustias to join the units already there. Ortiz had gotten her own picture of Castro and it was in the hands of each of her officers, whether they were going to Angustias or staying behind.

"How's Iris?" Sheriff Ortiz asked.

"She's back on the road with Gonzalo."

"After taking two shots? That's some girl you got yourself, Hector."

Hector didn't know exactly how to answer this. Of course, the sheriff was right, but he thought his love for Calderon had gone unnoticed. If the sheriff from another town, a person he met only once or twice a month, knew, then what were the chances Gonzalo had no idea? His pause forced Ortiz to speak again.

"Relax, Hector. Nobody cares if you two are seeing each other. You're not going on any kind of report and Gonzalo will never know about you two until one of you tells him."

"How do you know?"

"You light up every time you see her . . ."

"No, I mean how do you know Gonzalo won't find out?"

"He's a man. Men are dense. How long did it take you to realize that you loved Iris?"

"A year."

"Like I said. Men are dense. A woman like that, Hector? It should have taken you three minutes, four tops."

"Anything else?" Hector asked, and it was clear from his tone that he was getting off the subject of his love life and back onto the fugitive.

"Yeah, the guy also went after a former drug addict who's working as a mechanic at a garage near our border with you guys."

"A *former* addict? What's that?"

"He got religion. He's been clean for . . . let me see . . . two years now. We've checked him out a bunch of times, but he did his prison bit, he got Jesus, and he hasn't looked back."

"I'll believe it when I see it," Hector said.

"Don't be such a cynic. Anyway, your man is following a pattern. It might be a way to track him."

"I'll pass it along to Gonzalo," Hector said.

He left the other messages for the time being. Gonzalo could get to them if they needed getting to. At the moment, Castro's pattern made his movements seem predictable. If Castro stayed in Angustias, it would be to find the money. If Castro thought the dealers and drug addicts had the money, then Hector would talk to the dealers and addicts.

Seven people had been arrested for dealing drugs in Angustias in recent years, and Hector knew each one of them—he had arrested all of them at one time or another. Three of them lived in the same barrio. La Cola, the tail, was the poorest, least-developed section of Angustias. The barrio was splayed onto a hillside so steep there wasn't enough pressure to get water to most residents—it was trucked up and pumped into tanks instead. There were no street-lights and most residents had no phones; some had no electricity, lighting their homes with kerosene lamps. La Cola was a nightmare to search. Many houses had been abandoned, some before comple-tion; some driveways branched off the only road in La Cola only to get lost in the woods and die or end in a sheer drop off a cliff.

It was driving up into La Cola that Gonzalo called on the radio asking if Hector or anyone else had heard three shots. Hector answered that he had not and was told to go on with his business.

The first drug dealer Hector visited, Pablo Romero, denied ever having heard of Castro. Romero had done seven years in prison, getting out only recently. Hector was pretty sure the man was back into the business of selling drugs, since he had money to rent the house he lived in and had bought a used car. Still, if he was dealing, it wasn't in Angustias.

"How'd you get the black eye?" Hector asked.

"I don't know."

"Do you know how you got the bruise on your forehead? The one that looks like the muzzle of a gun?"

Romero put his hand to his forehead, fingering the bruise that marked where Castro had jabbed a gun in his face.

"I don't know that, either."

"Look, I can't protect you if you don't say anything. Tell me where he was headed. Was he going to see Bobby Valdez, maybe?"

The dealer laughed. "Protect me? You don't even know where this guy is. You had him in custody . . ." Romero held his hands out in front of himself as though he were in cuffs. "You had him and he got away. You think that was an accident?"

"What do you mean?"

"Look, let me tell you something. This guy, Castro? He's nothing. He's running around with a gun, he's shouting at people, he's looking for money. You caught him, he escaped. Who gave him the key? Catch him again, and he might escape again, or they might put a bullet in his head for being a *pendejo*. See what I mean?"

"Who? Who might put a bullet in his head?" Hector asked.

The dealer laughed again. He put his hand on the doorknob, preparing to go in and shut the door behind him.

"Who? Who gave him a gun in the first place, *chico*?" Hector stopped the door as it was closing. "Dominicans? Colombians?"

More laughter. Hector's guesses were apparently a highlight of the dealer's day.

"Man, you're just lost. Let me help you out a little. When you catch this guy, here's what you do, first you kill him—slow and painful if you ask me. Anyway, next, you check his gun. If it didn't come out of some police evidence locker, you bring it over here. I'll put a little salsa on it and eat it."

"Metropolitanos?"

"Metropolitanos, Municipales, DEA, FBI, NYPD—I've seen connections going every which way, *chico."*

"Follow the guns?"

"What can I say? Usually they say follow the money. You don't got the money. Follow the guns, then. Anyway, I got things to do," Romero said.

"What kinds of things?"

"Legal ones," he said, then he shut the door.

Hector stood outside and made notes of everything that seemed important from this conversation and many things that did not. If this dealer was anywhere near the truth, the investigation was just beginning, and though he had faith in his sheriff, he didn't see how it would be possible for any one man to trace the guns as far as the dealer had suggested.

Gonzalo called him over the car radio; he leaned through the passenger-side window to pick up the CB.

"Meet me at the station house," the sheriff said.

"I'll see you there."

While Gonzalo was driving away from Primavera's house, Captain Montalvo and Miguel Belen were putting their heads together in conversation.

"What exactly happened here?" Montalvo asked. "The truth."

"The truth? The truth is that stupid punk, Castro, shot the mayor, and I shot Castro. Easy."

"Which gun shot which man?"

Belen pointed with his cigar hand.

"This is my gun, this one belongs to Castro."

"Your gun is registered to you?"

"Of course."

"You usually bring it to the mayor's house?"

"When there's a crazy guy running around shooting people."

"Castro was in custody until just a while ago."

"Look. When Primavera and I left the *alcaldia,* that Castro guy was still running around with a gun. Ask Gonzalo. He's the one that told us to be prepared. Is this going to be a problem?"

"No. No problem."

"Good. Remember, I'm a hero. If people ask you, reporters or whatever, I'm a hero. Start saying it now, none of this, 'We have to finish the investigation to see what happened,'" okay? I'm a hero, and I'm the mayor of this town now. People have to know that what I say, goes. I don't bluff, I don't negotiate, I'm not Primavera. When I take out a gun, it's to shoot. When I shoot, I kill. Got that?"

"I got it," Montalvo said. "What about your sheriff?"

"Gonzalo? What about him?"

"Is he going to call you a hero? Or is there going to be trouble there?"

"Gonzalo's on vacation starting tomorrow. He's typing up a report for you on what he knows. He'll be giving you the evidence he collected, testimony, things like that. He'll be typing until his plane leaves."

"And you're sure he's not going to cancel his flight?"

"I think I got the message across. This is your investigation, Montalvo. Don't mess it up."

Montalvo motioned Rivera to his side.

"Get the camera and the lockbox from the trunk. Bring the dust kit."

"We're dusting for prints?" Rivera asked.

Montalvo shot him a look.

"Okay, okay. Lockbox, camera, dust kit." Rivera headed down the stairs.

"Are you dusting for prints?" Belen asked.

"You said not to screw up the investigation. There's a mayor dead here along with a guy who has killed a bunch of people, and that's just counting the ones from today. The press is going to be all over this sooner or later, and I'm not going to tell them I didn't collect evidence."

The cooling night air hung between the two men while they waited for Rivera to return. There was no breeze. Primavera had a short-cut grass lawn running wide all around the house. This cut down on the bug life that could be heard. Still, there were owls and bats in the woods making their noises, and in the distance there were dogs answering each other blindly from farms on different hills.

"You want to do prints or camera work?" Rivera asked, returning from the car.

"Camera."

"Where do I take the prints from?"

"Handrail," Montalvo said.

Montalvo took photos of Primavera from different angles while Rivera worked on the railing. He moved over to take photos of Castro on the stairs.

"Anything?" he asked Rivera before heading back to the balcony.

"What? Prints? Nothing useful. A lot of smudges. A lot of partials, and even if one of these belongs to Castro, it only proves he was here."

"It proves we didn't plant him here," Montalvo answered.

"What?"

"We didn't plant him. We didn't kill him somewhere else and plant him here."

"Who would say that?"

"The press. You know how they are. They'll say anything. This is a mayor. When this gets out, there'll be theories all over the news. Trust me."

"But fingerprints don't prove anything," Rivera said. "If we moved the body, why wouldn't we plant the prints, too?"

"It's corroboration. Just get the prints."

When he was satisfied with his collection of photos, Montalvo put the camera down and took up the lockbox and moved to the chair with the guns.

"What's the plan?" Belen asked.

"Watch."

He opened the box, pulled out a gun, put Castro's gun in, and closed the box again. He fired the gun over the balcony railing into the clay dirt of the lawn.

"I don't get it."

"It was Rivera's gun," Montalvo said, pointing to the lockbox. "No one has to know that it was used here."

"What about the slug?"

"Through the sternum. The lead should be mush."

"Should be?"

"Relax. We have a man in the coroner's office."

"What about my gun?" Belen asked.

"What about it? Your gun is yours. You're a hero, remember?"

Belen smiled and gave the captain a pat on the back.

"How would you like to be the next sheriff of Angustias?" he asked.

"Not for all the money in—"

Both men heard a scraping noise from around the balcony corner. Faint as the sound was, they were both sure they heard it. They looked at each other but didn't bother with calling out "Who's there?" They headed toward the origin of the sound. Someone whispered, "Shit," loud enough for them to make out, and sprinted away from them.

There were stairs at the far end of this side of the balcony that let out to the rear of the house. Lucy Aponte took the stairs two by two, jumping the last five to the grass. She moved quickly, but Montalvo had longer legs and had made up some of the distance between them. She started to run around to the front of the house, she wanted to get to the road, where she had left her car, but Rivera had been alerted to the chase and blocked her path. She veered away from him and away from her car and toward the woods.

It was a straight run across the neatness of the lawn to the tangle of trees. Montalvo began to fade behind her, and Rivera never really got close. She knew that if she made it into the woods, they would have to stop chasing her. Only an acre or two of trees separated her from the next house. She chanced a quick look over her shoulder. Montalvo was putting more effort into each stride, but slowing; Rivera had given up and was jogging; Miguel Belen was on the lawn, a gun held in front of him taking careful aim at her. He fired and she fell on the grass, skidding a yard before hopping back to her feet. She assured herself that she hadn't been hit—fear had taken her off her feet when she heard the crack of the gun firing.

"Don't make me kill you!" she heard Belen yell, and having seen all she had seen and heard all she had heard that night, she thought it wise to come to a stop where she was and put her hands above her head. She didn't turn around as the officers came up behind her. She stared into the woods only twenty more yards away. She felt the smack of metal on the top of her head and the woods were dark to her by the time she hit the ground.

CHAPTER TWENTY

Gonzalo arrived in front of the station house a few minutes after Hector, and he arrived alone. Iris Calderon could hardly keep her eyes open, so he had driven her back to the clinic. She could sleep in relative peace there, and he promised to pick her up at eight-thirty in the morning, right after her breakfast.

He slumped into the chair at the side of his desk, the one he usually reserved for suspects and victims to sit in while he took down their information. He knew he wasn't a victim, but he certainly didn't feel like being the sheriff. A headache was beginning to grab him by the neck again, and even though he had eaten well less than two hours before, he was as hungry as he had ever been in his life. He made a mental note to request one of those candy machines for the station house.

Hector was seated at the only other desk in the room, rifling back and forth through the notes he had made.

"Anything new?" Gonzalo asked.

Hector held up a finger asking his boss to wait a moment as he made sense of his own handwriting.

"Well, I've got something new," Gonzalo said.

Hector looked up.

"Guess who's dead now."

"Castro?"

"Yup, Castro and Primavera."

Hector's eyes widened and he tilted his head back to take in the information.

"They killed each other?"

"Almost. The story goes that Castro came to Primavera's house, killed Primavera, and Belen killed Castro."

"The story?"

"Belen's the only witness left alive. For all I know he killed them both. Or maybe Primavera killed Castro and Belen killed Primavera."

"Why didn't you get me on the radio?" Hector asked. "There's work to do. We can figure out who shot who—"

Gonzalo held up a hand.

"We're off the case," he said.

"What does that mean?"

"It means we're going to type up reports, turn over evidence, and go to sleep. Montalvo and Rivera are running things now."

"Our mayor gets killed and we sit on the sidelines?"

"Yup."

"Whose idea was that?"

"There's a new mayor in town, Hector. Besides, there are homicide detectives here, too."

"But they're crooked."

"Do you have any proof of that? Let me know, and I'll call internal affairs. Hell, I'll arrest them myself."

The two men sat in silence a moment contemplating the death of their case.

"Can we follow up on the evidence we've collected already?" Hector asked.

"If you have a lead, we'll follow it, but I'm pretty much dry."

"Well, let me tell you about my conversation with Sheriff Ortiz."

Gonzalo was attentive to Hector's report concerning Ortiz's information and his conversation with Pablo Romero in La Cola. He wasn't surprised by the wild allegations. Dealers often made allegations of police corruption, and it was rare when the President of the United States and even the Pope were left out of the picture. If Gonzalo were to start investigations against everyone drug dealers thought were complicit in the drug trade, there wasn't a single person in the world he wouldn't talk to sooner or later.

"What do you think?" Hector asked at the end of his story.

"I think that even if we were to put Pablo Romero on the stand in front of a grand jury, all we would accomplish is to get Montalvo and Rivera angry and ourselves thrown off the force."

Hector had no answer for that.

"Well, just so that you know. Maria Garcia called and so did Collazo and Lucy Aponte. Maybe they have something you can use." Hector handed Gonzalo the notes he had taken earlier.

"Well, I think I know what Aponte has," Gonzalo said. "Let me go pay Garcia a visit; this might be interesting. I'll call Aponte later."

"Want me to go with you?" Hector asked, getting out of his chair.

"Nope. I want you to start typing up your reports."

Gonzalo left the station house and crossed the plaza to Maria Garcia's house. It was past eight in the evening. He would have hesitated or called first if the visit were to almost any other citizen of Angustias, but Garcia was less formal than most, and her lights were on.

"Come on in," she said, leading the way in. Gonzalo closed the door behind him and followed her to her bar. She was in the same robe she had had on that morning.

"I thought you'd get back to me a little sooner," she said. She got behind the bar and made herself a drink. This time she didn't bother with offering one to Gonzalo.

"I've been a little busy," he said. "Is that the same robe you had on this morning?"

The lawyer ignored him.

"You asked for political dirt, and I think I hit the mother lode."

Gonzalo took out a notepad and pen.

"You got me curious, so I asked around about Primavera to see if any of my friends knew something I didn't."

The dramatic pause went on a little longer than Gonzalo could bear.

"And?"

"And there was nothing on Primavera. Miguel Belen, however, is not so clean. In fact, if you dig, I'm pretty sure you'll find he's about as crooked as they come. I put together a list of names—people you should look into—who got in trouble while Belen was nearby. I'm sure I can get twice as many names tomorrow."

Maria Garcia handed Gonzalo a half page of legal-pad paper with names and government positions, and then she went on to detail how Belen had started as a police officer in San Juan nearly twenty years before. He had been implicated in a minor scandal that Gonzalo vaguely remembered, and he had been forced to leave the department. In itself this was not damning. The department had gone through several scandals in a row, two of them quite major, and the decision was made to clean house. Officers who had even the slightest connection to the troubles were disciplined harshly. Many had been forced to retire in that same year. Those punished were not necessarily guilty. So far, this was not very important or interesting to Gonzalo.

"The important thing," Garcia said, "is what happened after he left the force. Instead of going down the ladder and out the door, Belen left his position and moved *up*."

"Up where?"

"A lot of different positions, but most of them have the same general description. He's always a liaison between the various levels of Puerto Rico's government and federal agencies—the DEA, FBI, *La Migra*, the Treasury Department, you name it."

Gonzalo thought about the information a moment.

"Any connection to scandals? Troubles?"

"Direct connections? None that I could find yet, but give me a few more hours tomorrow and that might change. What there is is a ton of scandals floating in the waters near him. There was the case of the shipment of two hundred kilos that the Coast Guard picked up in Ponce. He signed off on the transfer of the drugs as evidence to Florida. After the trial, the drugs went missing. It was one of the biggest busts and one of the biggest thefts of evidence."

"Still, this doesn't really—"

"There's plenty more. Remember when Judge Cardozo was murdered a few years ago? Belen was the only witness. Apparently in the office late at night briefing the judge about extraditions requested by *los federales,* some guy walked in, started shooting, Belen struggled for the gun and shot the guy in the thigh; he was gunned down a few blocks away. It didn't do the judge any good. That's the biggest scandal Belen has a connection with."

Gonzalo sat thinking about whether he should reveal the circumstances of Castro's death. The similarity of the current case with the one from some years ago had to be more than coincidence. The circumstances of Primavera's death would come out soon enough, he decided.

"Keep digging. Get me more of the same. Get me names," Gonzalo said.

"Well, can it wait till morning?"

"Not if you can get something right now. Think of it as a priority."

"Remember, Gonzalo, I'm not one of your deputies. It's late now and—"

"What you've told me so far makes Belen a murder suspect in my mind. I can't say too much more than that just yet."

"Murder? Who?"

"Francisco Primavera," Gonzalo said, getting up to leave.

"He's dead?"

"Yup. And Belen is the new mayor, and he's taking control of the investigation with the help of the *Metropolitanos,* Rivera and Montalvo. Call judges, call district attorneys, call politicians. Get in their faces. Get the information."

"This might stir up a hornets' nest," Garcia said. She was smiling and knew what he was going to say before he said it.

"I'm counting on it."

Hector was typing when Gonzalo got back to the station house. He looked up and saw the smile on his sheriff's face. He knew the case was back in Angustias hands; he hoped it would mean a quick end to the typing. He listened while Gonzalo called Sheriff Ortiz of Naranjito at her home number.

"What's up?"

"I need you to help me work this case here. I need you to get information on Miguel Belen, the mayor of Angustias."

"Mayor? What happened to Primavera? He quit?"

"He died. Bullet through the chest."

"Wow. You guys are having a really bad day over there, huh?"

"Yup, and I think I know who's ultimately responsible. Anyway, get out some paper and a pencil; I need you to check on these guys as soon as possible."

"Why don't you just fax me at the Naranjito station house? I'll go over and make my calls there."

"Fax you?" Gonzalo said, looking to his deputy for help. Hector got out of his seat and took the list of names from Gonzalo's hand. "Sure."

Gonzalo repeated the Naranjito fax number out to Hector who sent the document on its way.

"Listen Susana, the people you're calling may not want to talk to you, but I need you to push on this. If Belen is the type of man I think he is, he's connected. We're looking to see who has the worst reaction to the questions."

"Got it. You're looking to cause trouble. Don't worry; you'll get plenty. I know a couple of these people. I'll call you back in a couple of hours with a progress report."

Gonzalo thanked her for the assistance and hung up. He looked at his watch and found that a couple of hours would put him past ten. He called his wife to let her know what type of schedule he was on.

"What's the plan?" Hector asked as Gonzalo got off the phone.

"The plan," Gonzalo said, "is to look for trouble."

"Where do we start?"

"Oh, I think I know where trouble is. We've got a little more work to do, then we're going up to the Primavera house."

Gonzalo had Hector bring out the handguns Castro and Daniel had used on the Ortiz property. The serial numbers on both guns had been almost completely filed away, but Gonzalo was able to read them clearly enough with a magnifying glass. His theory was that criminals who thought they could never be caught as a matter of principle did the most careless jobs in covering their tracks, not understanding that it was a good job at covering their tracks that might keep them from getting caught. He had Hector fax Sheriff Ortiz these serial numbers as well.

"What next?" Hector asked. It was clear he wanted something to happen, some action.

"I need to return a couple of these calls." Gonzalo waved the little notes Hector had scribbled.

"It's a little late, isn't it?"

Gonzalo looked at the names on the notes. He put away two that he knew could wait until the morning. Messages from Collazo and Lucy Aponte might be professionally related and had to be answered. He called Collazo first. He answered on the first ring.

"Hey, Collazo, you still up?"

"Watching TV. Cristina is in bed already."

"Okay, you had a question for me?"

"It's about the Ortiz animals. What are you going to do with them?"

"What needs to be done?"

"Well, they need to be fed tomorrow, the pigs do. The cows need to be milked. Eggs should be collected . . ."

"Okay, I got it. Is there any way you can do this work? I'm sure Angustias would pay you for the work."

"I don't mind working with the other animals, but I hate pigs. They're disgusting. Besides, there's no more food for them."

"What do they eat?"

"Whatever doesn't move fast enough to get away."

"All right, can you go to the grocery store and buy them enough food for tomorrow?"

"If we can get a truck in through the Mendoza property, we can take all the animals to the butcher and sell them."

"We'll think about that tomorrow. I'll ask Maria Garcia what the law would say about that."

"Okay, I'll be there in the morning with a couple buckets of food."

Gonzalo wanted to tell his old friend of the shocking details he'd learned in the last half-hour, the death of the mayor, the possible complicity of the deputy mayor—but Collazo was no longer an officer of the law. Sharing this information would only be gossiping. He refrained from sharing what he knew and suspected.

Gonzalo's call to Lucy Aponte's home number got a busy signal. He tried again with no luck. He made a mental note to try again later in the evening but not too late.

"Are we going over to Primavera's now?" Hector asked.

"Nope. I'm going. First, I'll check with Jimenez, then Ramirez, then the Primavera house. You stay here. If Ortiz calls back with any good information, I want you to let me know. Also, get the Naranjito officers to check in with you. I didn't see any on the way here."

There wasn't any real reason to go to the Primavera house. He wasn't going to be arresting anyone just yet. He was going fishing. Maybe he could get them to implicate themselves. Maybe he could get them to confess to something just by annoying them. Maybe they'd apologize. At the very least, he'd be giving them the chance to do so. More importantly, like Hector, he wanted something to do.

Gonzalo got into his squad car and drove off. His first stop was at the Ortiz house. He got out of the car and walked to Jimenez, who was leaning against his car.

"Long night?" he asked.

"Yeah. All part of the job," Jimenez answered. He was trying to put a good face on a boring situation.

"Yeah," Gonzalo agreed. "You just got the part that stinks. Has anyone come by?"

"Some kids a while back. Nobody with any interest in the house."

Gonzalo shrugged and went back to his car. "I'll get you relieved in an hour or two, okay?"

It was Jimenez's turn to shrug.

The next stop was at the house of Rafael Ramirez. Ramirez was on the front porch with his wife. They were taking in the night air and shucking peas. Gonzalo didn't bother to get out of his car.

"How would you like to be mayor again, Ramirez?"

"Mayor? Of this town?"

"This town might need you soon."

"Why? That Primavera kid going to be arrested?"

"I can't tell you. All I can say is that the job might be open soon, and I'm sure the town would like your help."

"Angustias can go to hell."

"Every town has a time of crisis where they need someone to step forward, Ramirez. I think that time is coming for Angustias, and I think the man to step forward is you."

Ramirez waved him off, but Gonzalo knew his former and future mayor, and he knew Ramirez would be thinking about what he'd said. In the morning, he would be ready for the work. Gonzalo's next stop was the Primavera house.

CHAPTER TWENTY-ONE

Had Gonzalo known that Lucy Aponte was in police custody, chained to the ring bolt in the back of Montalvo's squad car, he would have approached Primavera's house quietly or called for Hector then created some diversion while his deputy freed the young reporter from her restraints. As it was, he didn't notice Lucy as he passed Montalvo's car, and his approach was almost unnoticed. She was bent over in her seat; the chain attaching her cuffs to the floor of the car had been knotted to make it shorter and her custody uncomfortable. The detectives and the mayor of Angustias were scouring the lawn with flashlights, stooping over. They all stopped as Gonzalo's headlights shone on them. They shaded their eyes, but didn't move toward the car or say anything. It was as though they were hoping Gonzalo would notice he had turned down the wrong driveway and back out.

"You guys lose something?" Gonzalo asked as he got out of the car. He addressed Montalvo who was nearest him, but Belen answered.

"Nothing you can help us with, Gonzalo. I thought you had reports to type out?"

Gonzalo waved the thought away with a smile.

"We're just about done with the reports. Just a few odds and ends to tie up. Nothing that won't keep until the morning." He pulled out his own flashlight and started sweeping the ground with its beams, though he had no idea what was being searched for.

"Well, then go get some rest. You have a big trip tomorrow," Belen insisted. "You probably have packing to do still."

"Ah, I can tell you're not a married man, Belen. Mari has had the packing under control for days. She wouldn't let me near the luggage to save her life. It's a pride thing, I think. According to her, I've never folded a piece of clothing correctly."

"Yes, well, you still have a lot of driving to do tomorrow and you have nothing to do here."

Gonzalo, and anyone else who might have been paying attention, could tell from his tone that Belen was suspicious of Gonzalo's arrival on the scene and wanted him to leave. Gonzalo kept searching the lawn. He pulled a pen from his shirt pocket and squatted. He picked up a copper casing and held it up to the light from his own flashlight. It was filled with red clay, dented and nicked in several spots. The three men looked at each other and then back at him.

"You see, I can recover evidence, too," Gonzalo said. Then he let the casing fall back to the ground. "Too bad I can't prosecute that crime."

"What crime is that?" Montalvo asked.

"New Year's. I told Primavera that as mayor he should set an example for the people of Angustias. 'Don't shoot off any guns,' I told him. He promised that he wouldn't, but there were complaints that they heard and saw him shooting a forty-five into the air. It's a silly tradition, and he should not have supported it. Still, I think we can all agree that he's beyond my reach now. Besides, if everyone who fired off a gun on New Year's got arrested, they'd have to build new prisons just for them. Anyway, there's about a half-dozen casings right here." He shone his light at the spot where he had picked up the first one. "Hey, since this is a crime scene, do you think we should collect these? You know, to exclude them?" He aimed this question at Montalvo and again Belen answered.

"I think you should get out of here and let us do our jobs, Gonzalo."

"Don't mind me. Search away. If you let me know what we're looking for, we can cover more ground."

"Look Gonzalo, you want to be helpful? Go finish your reports, gather your evidence, and bring it back here. That might be helpful."

"Well, it might take a while. I have some leads I'm still following, and we've collected a ton of evidence, ballistics, weapons, bloody clothing, things like that. It all needs to be cataloged properly. You know the drill. It might be a couple more hours."

"Take your time. We'll be here. Go. Catalog, collect, follow your leads."

"I think I'll do that," Gonzalo said. "I'll follow the leads and I'm sure I'll be seeing you again soon."

He turned off his flashlight and started to walk back to his car. The three men began to go over the lawn again with their lights. Gonzalo turned back, flashlight on and raised, shining out at eye level. He spotlighted Castro on the stairs to the balcony.

"Did the coroner say when they'd be able to make it over here to pick up the bodies?" He asked this as he moved toward the stairs. Belen moved to cut him off, shining his light into the sheriff's eyes.

"None of that is any of your concern now," he said.

"Don't worry," Gonzalo said, backing away, not wanting to spark a confrontation just then. "I'll call them for you."

"We already called," Montalvo said. He knew it was a mistake to lie and was sorry he had opened his mouth. He hoped Gonzalo would drop the subject.

"Did you call the guy in Ponce? He responds faster than most, especially at night."

"I called the guy in Caguas," Montalvo said, wishing he could stop the lying, but finding it a difficult thing to do once started.

"Ah, I don't know him at all," Gonzalo said. He too was lying, but then no one there wanted him to stay and explain or defend himself.

"Cover them," Gonzalo said, walking back to his car again.

"What?"

"Cover them," he repeated. "Find blankets and cover them. It's hot and humid. They've been dead for a while. There'll be flies soon enough. Cover them."

He opened his car door and got in. He sat for a while making notes into his notepad, checking his watch, and scribbling some more. The three men on the lawn studied his motions.

"I'll be back as soon as I can," Gonzalo called out his window. "Can I count on you for an update about what took place here?" he asked Montalvo. "You know, out of courtesy? After all, it is my town. I live here, and that's my mayor up there, dead."

"Not a problem, Sheriff. Just let us do our jobs in peace, and you will know everything we know as soon as we know it."

Gonzalo had put his car in reverse while Montalvo spoke and was already pulling away during the last few words, looking back over his shoulder and clearly not caring what the detective had to say about his plan for sharing information.

"He knows something," Montalvo said as the car rolled down the long drive. He was talking to Belen.

"He knows nothing," Belen answered. "I've never seen more desperate fishing in all my life."

"He may be fishing, but he knows what he's looking for. Everything we gave him, he threw back. He knows which fish is a keeper."

At the bottom of the drive, Gonzalo made a turn to get back onto the road front first. In making the turn he looked at the detectives' squad can just a few yards away. This time, he saw the head of Lucy Aponte as she looked through her left-side window. Her face showed up to her nose. There was a blade of grass in her hair and her eyes were wide with fear. A small corner of gray duct tape showed telling Gonzalo that if he could see her whole face, he'd find her mouth had been taped shut. In the second it took for him to pause cautiously before getting onto the road in front of the house, he looked directly into her eyes and gave her a slight nod, letting her know that he was aware of her trouble and would help her.

He got onto the roadway smoothly, and none of the men searching the grass had bothered to watch him leave or they might have seen the nod and Lucy Aponte's head showing itself.

Gonzalo drove quickly. He needed to inform Hector at least and hopefully several other officers of Lucy's predicament, but he didn't want to risk using his radio. Montalvo had one just like it. The drive to the station house was only a mile and a half, but much of it was filled with hairpin turns that earned the barrio the name of Las Curvas, the curves. There were also no street lamps to light the way. Minor roads in rural Puerto Rico rarely do have lamps; mountains make them difficult to place and maintain, and many residents move out to the country for peace and quiet that glaring lights in front of the house negate.

"Maria Garcia just called," Hector said, as Gonzalo rushed into the station house.

"Good, I'll call her back. Look, I need you to get to the Primavera house as fast as you can. Don't let them know you're there. Take my car, you're tailing Montalvo's squad car. They've got Lucy Aponte shackled in there. If they move the car, follow them. If they move Lucy, follow her. Don't let her out of your sight, got it?"

"What do they have her on?"

"She probably got in their way. Get out of here. I like Lucy. I'd like for her to make it out of this alive. Go, go."

Gonzalo shooed his deputy out the door with a wave and Hector went, taking Gonzalo's keys. A moment later, as he sat at his desk, Gonzalo heard his car come to life and peel away from in front of the station house. He pulled his Rolodex across the desk to him and flipped through, finding Maria Garcia's number. Normally, he would have made the short walk to talk with her personally, but his feet hurt just then, and besides, he reasoned, electricity would make it to Garcia's house faster than he ever could.

"I've made a few of the phone calls you wanted, and one of those people gave me another name, and I got something I think you want to hear."

"Let me have it."

"Remember Nestor Ochoa?"

The question was rhetorical in nature, of course. No one could forget the damage Ochoa had done two years earlier. Gonzalo had been happy to put him in prison for what turned out to be a short stay, ending with a sharpened screwdriver through Nestor's ear.

"Well, Ochoa was sent to that boat crash in Rincón that started this whole thing by his precinct commander, but the man who decided to call a precinct in San Juan, seventy-five miles away, instead of Mayagüez, much closer, was Miguel Belen's superior at the time. I guess some kind of chief liaison between PRPD and *los federales*, like the Coast Guard."

"Well, that's good, but I was hoping for—"

"I'm not done. My source tells me that on that night and on at least four other nights when boats loaded with immigrants from the Dominican Republic sank offshore, the superior was away on short vacations and Miguel Belen issued the orders. Each time, it was Ochoa's precinct that got the call no matter where the boat was, and each time Ochoa was sent out in the field. It was a game they played, Gonzalo."

"And who is this source?" Gonzalo asked.

"He worked in the same office. He was a little shy, especially once I told him that Belen is here and people are dying. I'll keep his name to myself for a while, if you don't mind."

"But at trial, I'll need a witness, not an unnamed source."

"First you have to get to a trial, Gonzalo. Also, don't forget you're not the prosecutor. Anyway, things get even better. This source kept track of things in the office because the superior was almost never actually in the office. He thought there might be a union grievance to file since everyone else had to essentially move up one rank in workload—Belen did his superior's work, the guy below Belen did Belen's work, et cetera. You get the idea. Everyone was working outside of their title and nobody was getting any extra pay. He kept notes, and he still has them. All the times Belen had to fill in for his boss."

"But he doesn't want his name revealed?"

"He says Belen scared the crap out of him, so I'm afraid he's going to need to see him in custody before he introduces himself."

"How'd Belen scare him? A threat or something?"

"It goes back to the Rincón incident. After the scandal hit the news, the source said he was going to tell somebody about the fact that his superior wasn't doing his job. When he talked to Belen, Belen told him that he knew where the missing body was—there were several bodies in the same place and his would be one of them if he didn't drop the issue. He wasn't sure whether to take Belen seriously or not, but his look said yes."

"He dropped it?"

"He dropped it and transferred out. He was that spooked."

"Okay. This helps. Keep digging."

"It's getting late, Gonzalo."

"Bill us for overtime. Angustias will pay," Gonzalo said before hanging up.

A few more flips through the Rolodex brought him the name of one of Lucy Aponte's editors from a daily newspaper in San Juan. The man had been to Angustias several times in the aftermath of Nestor Ochoa's attack on the town, coordinating the efforts of his writers and photographers as well as putting together his own columns on what was, for three weeks running, the biggest news event on the island. He had handed out his business card to several people in town; for Gonzalo he had added his home phone number on the back. Gonzalo called it now. The man who answered was clearly awakened by the call.

"Alvarez," he said.

"This is Luis Gonzalo, sheriff of Angustias here. I could use your help and I think I can help you as well. Can you speak?"

"Of course I can speak. Do you have any idea what time it is, Gonzalo?"

"Don't you reporters say that the news waits for no man?"

"No, we don't. What was it you wanted?"

"You have heard that a couple from Angustias were murdered, their house burned down?"

"Yes, of course. Lucy Aponte already reported on that—I think it was fourteen inches of column space along with two photos we got from her."

"There's more."

"More people died?" the reporter asked. Gonzalo could hear as he fished a cigarette out and struck a match.

"The guy who killed the family killed the mayor a little while ago."

"Jesus," Alvarez said. His voice was muffled a bit by a cigarette Gonzalo was sure was dangling from his lips. He was scribbling onto a piece of paper.

"How long ago was this?" Alvarez asked.

"Not positive on the specifics, roughly eight o'clock."

"And the mayor's name was?"

"Francisco Primavera. It gets worse."

"Uh-huh."

"The deputy mayor, Miguel Belen, shot and killed the man who shot Primavera."

"Uh-huh. No kidding? What are you guys running out there, the OK Corral?"

"It's not a laughing matter."

"No, no. You're right. And the name of the murderer?"

"Not yet available."

"Uh-huh. Okay. Uh, let me see. The mayor, Primavera, was gunned down. The killer, unidentified, was gunned down by the deputy mayor, Belen. Correct?"

"Yes."

"And Belen just happened to be at the right place at the right time?"

"That's why I'm calling you."

"Aha. I knew there was a catch. You have a capable journalist that lives right in your town, yet you're calling me. That's a little fishy, Gonzalo."

"Yes. Here's the problem, two problems in fact. First, Lucy Aponte is missing . . ."

"Oh my God, no."

"I'm afraid so. I strongly suspect she's in danger. And I also strongly suspect that the deputy mayor, Miguel Belen, was not in the right place at the right time by accident. It seems that he has a history of being in the right place at the right time whenever something bad is happening. I have a long list of people for you to track down and ask questions of."

Gonzalo started to read out his list of names that might have information of value to him, but Alvarez stopped him.

"Whoa, whoa. I can't just call up all these people in the middle of the night. What do you want me to ask them?"

"I want you to ask them about their relationships with Miguel Belen. I want you to dig for signs of corruption. I think he had something to do with the events of two years ago with Nestor Ochoa. I want to know about this connection. I think he may be part of a conspiracy to bring drugs into Puerto Rico along with illegal immigrants from the Dominican Republic. I want to know about that, too. If there is a conspiracy, I don't think he's the head of it. I want to know who is."

"And you want me to call people at ten at night and ask them about all this? Impossible."

"Nothing's impossible. Lucy Aponte's missing. I think she's in danger. She might wind up dead. I have ten more names to give you. Call everyone. Tell them I was the one who gave their names as people who might know something. If they get angry, it'll be with me."

Gonzalo wanted to explain to the reporter that he was being squeezed out of the investigation and that he wouldn't have the power to do anything at all for anyone including Lucy in just a few more hours. He stopped short of saying this. He didn't know what it would do to his credibility. Besides, he didn't have time for more conversation. There were other calls to make.

"Still," Alvarez said. "Shouldn't you try to build a more careful case? Besides, I'm not a police officer or detective. I'm a reporter."

"With a person in danger, I don't have time to build a case, Alvarez. Forget detective, forget reporter, be a hero. Shake the tree, Alvarez; the rotten fruit will fall."

After giving the editor all the names others had collected for him, Gonzalo still wasn't sure that Alvarez would be making the phone calls that were needed. He gave out his home phone number in case anything turned up in the middle of the night. He moved on to make one other call.

"Susana, please tell me you've come up with something on Belen," he begged the sheriff of Naranjito.

"Of course I have more information, but nothing you can really sink your teeth into just yet. There's a question about a dinghy Ochoa may have used on the night of the boat crash in Rincón. *Maybe* it was brought out of a police evidence warehouse. There's a question about a whole truckload of guns that were supposed to be destroyed. A truckload of marijuana, a truckload of counterfeit Mexican currency . . ."

"Mexican?"

"Let's say, your man Belen was around a lot of suspicious doings over the last ten years or more. Look, I've got a couple more calls to make, and I'm waiting for two property clerks, Ponce and Mayagüez, to call me back."

"You have them jumping through hoops for you?"

"I don't know about hoops, but one of them said it was his pleasure to go down to the station house and look through old files for something he thought he remembered about the Ochoa-Belen connection."

"He could get into trouble for being there out of his shift."

"He said that would be his pleasure, too."

"Gee, why don't they ever say things like that to me?"

"I don't know. Ask Mari. Got to go."

With that, Gonzalo sat back, looked at his watch to see how close to the new day it was, then flipped through the Rolodex again and again, calling the coroner of the Caguas office and a judge living in the same city. He got what he wanted from both, checked the contents of Hector's squad car trunk, got into the driver's seat, and drove out for a round of face-to-face visits. His first stop was the judge's home.

CHAPTER TWENTY-TWO

Pablo Jimenez, rookie officer, built something along the lines of a baby bull, had joined the police of Puerto Rico because he wanted to do good. Yet here he was on a day when several had been killed in town, when officers and civilians had been shot, guarding a house no one wanted to break into. He had been sitting in his patrol car for hours, stretching occasionally, yawning more frequently and once in a great while having a conversation with a local resident. He felt they must have come up to him out of pity; they seemed otherwise uninterested in what had gone on that morning.

Don Jose had come by several times during the waiting hours. He stood a foot or two from the squad car window with arms crossed, adjusting his black-rimmed glasses from time to time, unfolding his arms to use both hands to do so.

"Do you know who I think did it?" he asked the first time.

"Who?"

"The *Americanos*. There was one here a few months ago. I thought to myself, maybe this gringo wants to buy the farm. He talked to Pedro for an hour. He took fruits with him in his arms, like this." Don Jose cradled an imaginary baby.

"Did you hear what they were talking about?"

"It was English. I don't know English."

Not knowing what else to do with this conversation, Officer Jimenez spoke when it seemed clear Don Jose expected it of him and was happy when the old man left. In subsequent visits, Don Jose claimed to know that Pedro Ortiz had large debts—maybe a loan shark killed him—and that Pedro and his wife had been *Independistas,* Independence Party members who wanted Puerto Rico to break with the United States and become its own nation. The *Independistas,* Don Jose said, were only a step away from Socialists, and Socialists, it was well known, were capable of anything. Jimenez didn't know what to do with this lead either, but he made sure to write it down as he did with the others. He didn't intend to report any of it officially, but Don Jose wasn't going to be happy with a promise to remember the details of the information he gave; Don Jose wanted to see the notes being written.

When Don Jose got back to his house each time, he reported once again to his guests that the Angustias police were making no progress on the case except whatever progress he provided for them himself.

"They didn't even know these people were Independence Party people—that's only one step to being like Stalin," he said.

"Being Independence Party is bad enough," one of his guests said. "They kill people, too."

"You mean like Lolita Lebron?"

"And Albizu Campos."

"No. Now let's leave Albizu Campos out of all this." Don Jose drew a line at the most famous of all *Independistas,* Pedro Albizu Campos. It was clear that though the man was wrongheaded, his heart was in the right place.

From the driver's seat in his squad car, Jimenez also spoke to several children, including one boy who had decided to throw a rock at what was left of the Ortiz home. The only spark of excitement came for Jimenez when he recognized Carlos Velez walking past the car when, Jimenez thought, he should have been in a cell at the station house. He flashed on the roof rack of lights and used the radio as a PA system to get Carlos's attention and call him over to the car.

"What did you do, break out?" Jimenez asked.

"Gonzalo said he couldn't deal with me tonight. I'm supposed to go home and stay there until he comes to get me in the morning."

Given all that Jimenez had heard about Carlos being a regular customer at the Angustias station house, the officer thought it was probable that the story Carlos told was true. He took no chances, however, interrupting Gonzalo for a brief moment to ask about it via radio. Gonzalo confirmed the story and Jimenez sent Carlos on his way. That small incident was as close to excitement as Jimenez saw that evening. He sat considering transfer options.

When Gonzalo pulled up a little before midnight, the deputy was near to falling asleep.

"Why don't you get out of the car and take a little stroll? Get a little air into your lungs. You'll feel better."

"I'm fine, I'm fine," Jimenez started to protest, but a yawn escaped him as he finished his statement, so he got out of the car and shadowboxed for a second.

"Feel better?" Gonzalo asked.

"No."

"Well, I tried. Look, this may take a while longer. I'll try to get one of the officers from Naranjito to relieve you in another hour, okay?"

"I can stay awake."

Gonzalo looked at his deputy and for an instant he saw the face of a child rubbing the sleep out of his eyes, protesting that he is old enough to stay up with the adults.

"Here, let me get you relieved right now."

Gonzalo got on his radio and called for one of the Naranjito officers to come over to the Oritz house. He got an answer. One car with two officers would be there within five minutes. In the wait, Gonzalo spoke with his deputy.

"Anything interesting besides the Carlos incident?"

"Nope. Don Jose has been here a bunch of times, but not recently."

"Ah. What did he want?"

"He had a bunch of theories about who might have killed Pedro and his wife."

"You wrote it all down?"

"I had no choice. He wouldn't leave until I showed him my notes."

"Good. You never know when what looks like nothing will turn into something."

"Believe me," Jimenez said. "Don Jose's stories won't turn into anything."

"How about you believe me? You never know what piece of information will turn into something. Never."

Gonzalo went on to explain in brief detail all he had seen at Primavera's house, shocking the deputy with the news of the mayor's death and the death of the culprit and the detaining of Lucy Aponte.

"Any idea what they were looking for in the grass?" Jimenez asked as the Naranjito squad car parked in front of the Ortiz property.

"Oh, I have a pretty good idea what they were looking for. If they're arresting a photographer, they want her film. If she threw a roll of film into the woods, they won't be finding it until morning, if then."

"But if they kicked you off the case, they have all the time in the world, right?"

"Yup. But we're going over there now. We're going to tell them that time's up."

"We are?" Jimenez perked up at the prospect of something substantial to do.

"Yup. Just follow me and do exactly what I say."

As far as Gonzalo was concerned there were two ways he could handle the situation he was about to create. He could try to sneak up on the mayor of Angustias, turn his headlights off, or even show up in his own personal car. But this plan, he thought, had little chance of any real success. The large lawn around the Primavera property meant he would be seen from fifty yards away.

Instead, Gonzalo gambled that Belen would either not understand the nature of Gonzalo's third visit to the scene or not feel like resisting. He wanted to bring in more officers, but if the two detectives decided to put up a fight, Gonzalo thought it would be wisest to back away rather than fight, and he didn't know if he could easily control officers from Naranjito in what he thought would be a delicate task.

The men drove to the Primavera house. Gonzalo risked a radio call to Hector just to say that he was going to be in the area. Hector understood. The next minute was peaceful. As they approached Primavera's house, Gonzalo could see the detectives' squad car, and farther up the road, the front end of Hector's squad car peeking out of foliage. Detective Rivera was near the passenger side of the squad car, and Gonzalo decided to pull up snugly alongside the car that held Lucy Aponte, blocking access to the driver's-side door, making it near impossible for anyone to move the car without doing damage to both his car and theirs.

As soon as Gonzalo put his car in park, Rivera jumped into his car, turned the engine on, and began pulling out, Lucy Apoute still chained in the back. Gonzalo shifted into drive, trying to move up, but he was a fraction of a second too late and Rivera was too aggressive. Rivera pushed around the front of Gonzalo's car, turning it so that it was almost perpendicular to the road. By the time he righted himself, his car was crushed in the front right quarter and was minus one headlight. He picked up his radio.

"You got him, Hector?"

"I got him."

It turned out, Hector didn't have him. Rivera accelerated, clipping the front end of Hector's car, taking off his front fender cleanly, shooting it several feet into the woods by the side of the road. Hector fishtailed onto the road after Rivera. They were headed north, out of Angustias, into Naranjito and beyond that to the big cities and San Juan itself. Gonzalo sat in his car for a moment. He took a look at the two men who were left on the lawn, Belen and Montalvo. They appeared to be talking to each other calmly. He radioed the sheriff of Naranjito to let her know what was headed her way. She promised a roadblock since there was one marked car traveling that road. They just couldn't do anything more than a one-car block with such short notice. Gonzalo understood. He also trusted that there was no one on the island who could outrun Hector in a car chase. *Especially now that he has less fender weight,* he thought to himself as he stepped out of his car.

He brought the car back onto the grass in front of Primavera's house, his fender scraping up dirt while in reverse and smoothing it out in drive. Gonzalo got out and Jimenez mirrored him. The sheriff took a quick look at the damage to his car, moving slowly since the new mayor and Montalvo seemed in no hurry.

"You guys find what you were looking for?" he asked, walking up to where Belen was. Belen ignored the question.

"What the hell was that I saw, Gonzalo? Didn't I ask you to leave? Don't you have other work to do?"

"I did a lot of it," Gonzalo said. "I just have a little more that I have to say to you here before I can finish for the night."

"Like what?"

"Like you're under arrest as an accessory to the attempted murder of Officer Roberto Ramos, Officer Hector Pareda, and Raul Ruiz, store owner."

"You're crazy," Belen said. The words came out sounding calm, but Gonzalo could tell that the new mayor was seething. Repressing those words would have meant biting his tongue and drawing blood.

"I'm not the only one," Gonzalo said, pulling a folded warrant out of his pants' back pocket. "Judge Ramos thinks you should be arrested, too. Something about giving Castro a shotgun and lying about it to me.

"Cuff him," he said to Officer Jimenez.

Jimenez took the hand cuffs from his gun belt and reached out to grab the mayor's right wrist. Belen was surprised by the move, and when he felt his wrist firmly in Jimenez's hand, he tried to pull it away. Jimenez was a much stronger man than Belen had ever been and he pulled back, forcing Belen a step closer. That was when Belen snapped and threw a punch at the deputy's head. He missed, but Jimenez didn't miss in slapping Belen to the ground with a forearm to the head. He turned the mayor onto his stomach and forced both wrists into the cuffs.

"You guys are crazy!" Belen yelled, lifting his head off the ground to do it.

"Yeah, but we're not going to jail for resisting arrest," Gonzalo said.

"Should I put him in the car, boss?"

"Nope. Not yet. He had a gun on him earlier. Make sure it's not on him now. Then wait right here with him. I have another warrant." He pulled more paperwork out of his back pocket and offered it to Detective Montalvo. Montalvo glanced at it and handed it back.

"You think we are incapable of searching the premises?"

"I don't know. I saw the three of you out here with flashlights. That didn't inspire the most confidence. Anyway, as I explained to Judge Ramos, I think you and Rivera are involved in the killings that went on here."

"That's ridiculous. You were on the scene here before us. Have you lost your mind?"

"I don't mean the killings on this property alone. I mean in Angustias. Anyway, read the warrant. We're looking at this property and all the vehicles on it including your squad car, specifically named. Having Rivera move it only makes my job more difficult, not impossible."

Montalvo snatched back the warrant and read it more carefully.

"Now you can help me," Gonzalo said. "Or you can just step out of the way and let me find whatever there is to find."

Montalvo thought for a half minute. He agreed to help.

"Where do you want to start?" he asked.

"How about we start by talking about Lucy Aponte and what she was doing here?"

"How do you . . ." Montalvo started, but he thought it would be better to admit Lucy's presence.

"I have no idea why she was here. We arrested her for criminal trespass."

"On what grounds? Don't tell me Primavera made out a complaint."

"It's a crime scene."

"There's still not tape up to indicate that. She might have been on the property legitimately."

"She ran when we told her to stop."

"Which way was she headed?"

Montalvo pointed out toward the road.

"That doesn't make much sense, Montalvo. She was trespassing so you arrested her for trying to get off the property quickly. No difference. If she was running to the road, that means she was at the house. Where was she when you first saw her?"

"What does this have to do with Primavera's murder?"

"Do you want to help or get out of the way?"

"Go to hell, Gonzalo. I'm getting out of the way."

"That's fine by me. The way I figure, if she saw the murders, then she was probably on the balcony somewhere. I'm guessing just around that corner there." He pointed. "So she could take pictures through those two windows without being easily seen."

Gonzalo was speaking as though thinking out loud for the benefit of the detective. He started for the stairs up to the balcony.

"You guys were probably looking for film or audiotape which she probably would have put in one of the potted plants on that side of the balcony," he said. "Oldest trick in the book—Agatha Christie, that sort of thing."

Montalvo started after him. Gonzalo stepped over Primavera's body on the balcony floor and headed for the far right-hand corner. Montalvo was only a step behind him.

"See, from this corner, behind this plant, she would be in the shadows, and"—he squatted where Lucy had been less than an hour before—"she could take photos through this window. This gives her a line of sight through the windows on the adjacent wall."

Gonzalo used his right hand to show how the angles of vision available to someone in that position allowed for a wide view of the front of the balcony where the shooting had taken place.

"In fact," he continued, "Lucy's so small that she could probably even leave this corner, lie on her belly, and hide behind this pot over here."

He pointed to another large potted plant against the wall on the front side of the balcony. He moved the pot slightly, making a scraping noise Montalvo recognized.

"And look, Lucy Aponte's portable phone. It has a little green light on. I assume that means it's working. Who do you think is listening on the other side? Whoever it is must have gotten an earful. The phone's only, let me see, about eight feet from Primavera's body.

"You look shocked, Montalvo. What's the matter? Didn't you think a woman could be smart enough to track your moves? Or is it that you didn't think some hick cop could figure you out?

"Look at this pot over here."

Gonzalo stood and rounded the corner again. He took out his flashlight and pointed its beam at the dirt in the pot. There was a small mound on the surface.

"Something's buried here."

Gonzalo dug out a handful of dirt. He revealed the black plastic of a film container. He stood up and faced Montalvo.

"If you guys had taken the time to think about where to look instead of chasing her and cuffing her, you would have found this stuff yourselves. You could have made a bonfire with it if you're as dirty as I think you are. Or you could have used it against Aponte if she really was doing something illegal."

Montalvo had nothing to say to this. Gonzalo stepped to the balcony railing and yelled down to Jimenez.

"Get Belen in your squad car. Chain him to the ring bolt. Bring up some evidence bags."

Jimenez gave him the A-OK sign and hoisted Belen to his feet, guiding him to the car by an upper arm. Gonzalo turned back to Montalvo and found a gun in his face.

"There's still time for a bonfire, Gonzalo."

Gonzalo had had guns aimed at him before, but never from inches away. It was an unpleasant experience. In the second before he said anything to the detective, Gonzalo reasoned that there was only a slim chance that the man would shoot. After all, shooting wasn't likely to help him get out of this jam, and Jimenez was still only a few dozen yards away.

"Tell me what your plan is," Gonzalo said. He didn't think Montalvo was going to share any plans, but he wanted to buy himself time until Jimenez made his way back.

"I'm going to take that film and burn it. Then I'm going to take your squad car and drive away. If you don't bother me, I won't bother you. You understand?"

"Sure."

Montalvo pressed his gun into Gonzalo's cheekbone as he used his free hand to get Gonzalo's gun from out of his holster. He tucked it under his arm and reached into Gonzalo's shirt pocket for the car keys.

"Got everything?" Gonzalo asked.

"Almost," Montalvo answered. Then he slammed Gonzalo across the top of his baseball cap with the barrel of his gun, sending him to the floor, making his world lose focus.

CHAPTER TWENTY-THREE

Hector Pareda drove the turns of Angustias's hills every day of the week, and he usually took the curves and straightaways, the dips and rises far faster than advisable. There was no trouble in staying close to Rivera in his squad car; Hector got to within inches, and stayed there except for those places where Hector knew Rivera would have to slow down to stay on the road. The only way Rivera could have escaped Hector's pursuit was to plow head-on into a tree and leave this world for the next. Though the chase speeds rarely exceeded eighty miles an hour, Hector's main concern was to keep Rivera from doing just that. He steered with one hand while using his radio, trying to get Rivera to slow down. The hill roads were not for the inexperienced.

"Rivera, Rivera, where are you going?" he asked.

Rivera never took a hand off the steering wheel to answer Hector. He couldn't.

"If you pull over near the mango tree, we can talk calmly," Hector tried. Rivera sped up.

From time to time, Hector could see the top of Lucy's head as she tried to sit herself upright to see where she was going. At least she was alive.

"Where are you going?" Hector asked again when Rivera failed to make a turn that would have taken him out of Angustias. Instead, he continued on a road that would take him back toward Angustias if he stayed on it. Rivera didn't stay with the road. He noticed his mistake and made another turn back in the direction of San Juan. Right direction, wrong road. Rivera was on a dead-end street. It would wind its way uphill through a half mile of curves and end at a wooden shack recently inherited by a young man who lived in New York. Hector knew this.

"You're going the wrong way, Rivera," Hector said, though he knew he wasn't going to be believed.

Rivera kept going as fast as he could handle the turns. Hector slowed, knowing there was nowhere for him to go. When he got to the shack, Rivera swerved to avoid it. The squad car went into a skid, rolling onto the driver's side. The skid continued onto the grass, past the shack. The car righted itself on a sharp decline, rolling backward ten feet, slamming trunk-first into a quenepa tree.

Hector pulled to a stop at the top of the decline, his headlights shining above the wreck. Rivera tried working the accelerator, but his car had nothing to give. He worked his way out of his seat and out of the car. He reached for his gun and fumbled with it. Hector pulled out his and aimed for Rivera's chest. The move made Rivera leave his gun alone. He started to climb his way to Hector, and Hector backed away from the precipice edge, giving him space to make his way to the paved road again.

"Take your gun out with your left hand, thumb and forefinger only," Hector said. "If you move quickly, I'll kill you."

Rivera did as he was told, holding the gun out in front of him as though he were holding a dead rat by the tail.

"Put it on the ground, and take two steps to me."

When Hector was satisfied, he holstered his gun and stepped up to Rivera. Rivera swung out a fist badly, hitting nothing as Hector took a step back. With Hector's step forward again, he caught Rivera between the eyes with a right hook that made him take a stutter-step back. Rivera landed on his ass, his hands on the ground behind him, supporting his weight. Hector kicked out one of those hands, rolled Rivera to his stomach, and cuffed his hands behind his back. He frisked the man, shoved him into the backseat of his squad car, attached him to the ring bolt on the floor, and secured the gun in the trunk. He did all this as quickly as he could. He wanted to get to Lucy, but if Rivera was feeling homicidal, he couldn't be allowed to act on those feelings.

When he made his way down to the wrecked squad car, Lucy was trying to leverage herself out of the steeply inclined car. Her hands were still cuffed and chained to the ring bolt, but the bolt was no longer attached to the car floor. Her wrists were bleeding, but not broken. There were bruises on her forehead and around her left eye, and the duct tape was still covering her mouth.

Hector undid the cuffs for her, asking her if she was injured. She shook her head. She tried undoing the tape, giving a hard pull as though she were waxing her legs, but the tape only uncovered an inch or two of her skin while causing her exquisite pain. She walked up the hill to Hector's car and tried to undo more of the tape, rolling it onto itself so that it didn't reapply itself on her face. She used two hands, one to hold back her skin and the other to peel the tape away, and stopped when she got an inch of her lips free.

"Clinic," she mumbled.

"Trust me, I was going to take you there without you torturing yourself," Hector answered.

Hector drove to the junction of the dead-end road and the road leading back toward Angustias and radioed for the Naranjito police to send a car his way. The one that had been waiting for the car chase to come his way responded and was there in under five minutes. Hector sent him to the top of the hill to secure the wrecked squad car.

"Don't let anyone near it. It has evidence and probably some weapons in it."

"I know what secure the site means," the Naranjito officer said. Hector was about to apologize for having stated the obvious, but the officer had already driven off to do his duty.

Hector drove the few minutes to the clinic with Lucy glaring at Rivera the whole way. When they stopped at the clinic's front door, Hector put on the siren and lights of the car to get the staff's attention. Dr. Perez came out.

"Are you still here?" Hector asked.

"Well, I can't sleep anyway." The cause of the insomnia was the missing Volkswagen.

Perez ushered Lucy to the clinic door, but she walked in under her own power.

"What about the officer?" Perez asked.

"How about you?" Hector asked, looking into his rearview mirror. Rivera shook his head. "Refusing medical treatment?"

"Yes," Rivera said.

"Wait here," Perez said. "I have a form for you to sign."

Perez went in. Hector tried raising Gonzalo on the radio, but he got no answer.

At Primavera's house, Detective Montalvo hurried to dig out the film containers from the plant pot. There were two of them and a small audio cassette in the dirt. He collected his lockbox of guns, evidence bags, the dusting kit Rivera had left behind, and his flashlight. His hands were full, and the lockbox and Rivera's flashlight were tucked under his arms. His hope was to walk right past Jimenez unnoticed; as far as Montalvo was concerned, Jimenez could find Gonzalo anytime after he'd left the scene with the evidence. The sheriff would have a big headache and he would have learned a lesson, but he wouldn't pursue a matter he couldn't prove. Since the main body of proof would be getting into the car with him and driving away, his only concern was making it to the car.

"Do you need help with that?" Jimenez asked. He was walking up to the foot of the stairs as Montalvo was headed down.

"Yes," Montalvo said. "Gonzalo said I should take his car into town to store some of this evidence."

"Well, I have to go to town to lock up the mayor. You want me to drive this in for you?"

"No, no. If you can just help me get to the car, I would appreciate it."

Jimenez jogged up a couple of stairs as Montalvo came down past Castro's body. He reached for the lockbox, taking it by its handle. Montalvo first released it from under his arm, but then thought better of having the Angustias cop handle the most sensitive evidence. He squeezed the box with his arm again as Jimenez was pulling it away. The end result of this hesitation was the lockbox falling to the stairs, coming unlocked, and spilling its contents.

Jimenez stared at the guns on the stairs, recognized a department-issue revolver among them, looked up at Montalvo, and got hit across the face with Rivera's flashlight. Montalvo had decided that his best bet of making a getaway now that the evidence was out was to knock out Jimenez as he had Gonzalo. Hitting Jimenez with the flashlight did nothing to further this plan. Having slapped Jimenez, he reared back to unleash as powerful a backhand with the flashlight as he possibly could. Jimenez, a couple of steps below him, pulled at one of Montalvo's ankles, knocking him onto his back on the stairs next to Castro. Montalvo struggled to get up, to get his leg out of Jimenez's hands. Jimenez pulled him down the rest of the stairs to the parking landing.

On a flat surface at last, Montalvo kicked Jimenez in the left shin with his heel. Jimenez let him go momentarily, giving him time to get up. Montalvo would have been wise to use this moment of surprise to put distance between himself and the much larger and younger officer, but he was still thinking of knocking Jimenez out, collecting his evidence, and making his escape. Jimenez, a half foot taller and seventy muscular pounds heavier, had now been hit hard twice. He decided to hit back. He grabbed the detective by the throat. The detective grabbed the choking hand with both of his, making the attachment more secure. Jimenez hooked his leg behind Montalvo's, driving him into the asphalt. For good measure, he lifted Montalvo a few inches and ground him into the pavement again. At this point, Montalvo recognized his escape fantasy for what it was and offered no more resistance.

Jimenez cuffed one wrist, looped the cuffs through the iron railing at the bottom of the stairs, and cuffed the other wrist. He patted Montalvo down, confiscated the gun strapped to his ankle, took off his gun belt, and called out for his sheriff. He took the stairs two by two and found Gonzalo still lying where the detective had left him.

Jimenez pinched Gonzalo's cheeks to wake him, and the sheriff opened his eyes in a few seconds.

"Montalvo?" he asked.

"I got him in cuffs."

"Good work, rookie."

"Okay. What do I do next?"

"Leave me here. I'll stand up in a minute. Go to the squad car.

Get Hector on the radio. Let him know what's been happening. See if you can get a squad car from Naranjito to come by."

"Then what?"

"Then we wait," Gonzalo said.

He checked the top of his head for blood and found enough to tell him stitches were in his future. Jimenez went to do all he had been told.

EPILOGUE

With stitches in his scalp and reports still to be typed out, Gonzalo slipped under the covers of his bed at four in the morning. This did not stop Mari from getting him up at seven.

"You've got work to do, don't you? You'll sleep on the plane," she said.

Gonzalo sat on the side of the bed, hoping for a reprieve, his arms feeling like lead, his body feeling like it had been beaten with sticks. He pointed to the small bandage covering his new stitches. Mari noticed it for the first time and seemed moved for a moment.

"How many stitches?" she asked. There was tenderness in her voice and eyes and she moved a hand to touch the spot where he had been injured.

"Two," he said, and her sympathy dried.

"You've had worse," she said, walking away. "Get dressed."

Gonzalo got into uniform, read over his notes at the breakfast table, and went out to pick up Iris Calderon from the clinic. There was a squad car in the parking lot already.

Inside, Gonzalo went to see Officer Ramos first. With a full-fledged concussion, his injuries were the most severe. His room was empty. Gonzalo approached a nurse.

"Ramos woke up at dawn and said he wanted to go home. We let him go an hour ago," she told him.

He crossed to Calderon's room and knocked. Hector was inside. He had brought over a change of street clothes and Iris was in them already.

"Are you ready to go home?" Gonzalo asked.

"More than ready. Hector said he'd take me."

"Of course," Gonzalo said. "And I want you to take your full seven days off. Department regs don't give you much, but they give you that at least."

He motioned for Hector to step out of the room with him.

"Before I leave, I'll set it up to get coverage from the departments around Angustias. It's your job to prioritize and balance everyone's schedule. Talk to the crime scene people every day without fail. We're the top priority, and we need them to remember that. The DA will be calling you, no doubt. Make time to talk to him."

"What are the charges going to be against these guys?"

"Everything. I'll be filing a report before I go. You'll see. Don't forget to finish your report as well, and get paper out of everyone, Ramos, Iris, Jimenez, the Naranjito guys, Collazo, Maria Garcia . . ."

"Everyone."

"Right."

The charges against Rivera, Montalvo, and Belen ranged from tampering with evidence to the assaults on Lucy Aponte, Gonzalo, and

Jimenez. Belen was charged as an accessory to attempted murder for Castro's rampage with the shotgun. Belen, Montalvo, and Rivera were charged as accessories to the murder of Francisco Primavera. Belen was also charged with the murder of Fidelio Castronueves.

The evidence for all of this was irrefutable. Lucy had followed Primavera and Belen to the mayor's house and started taping their conversation. She started photographing as soon as Castro showed up—one particularly effective photo showed Belen aiming at Castro, who had his hands down. The next shot caught smoke leaving the muzzle with Castro beginning to slump. Murder had never been more clearly caught on film. When her audio cassette finished, she called her own answering machine from her portable phone. This tape was of a much inferior quality, but it captured everything needed to show Montalvo was no less complicit in the crimes of the day. The tapes revealed that Primavera had been a puppet, under the control of Belen, but they did not show who Belen answered to, only that he did answer to someone.

Gonzalo left the case in the hands of the district attorney, presenting him with evidence and information collected by Lucy's editor, Maria Garcia, Sheriff Ortiz, and his own deputies. By the time he left the station house in the late afternoon, the connection between Belen and Montalvo going back a half-dozen years was becoming clear. Circumstantially at least, they seemed involved in more than a fair share of evidence going missing from evidence rooms, witnesses disappearing or refusing to testify in drug cases, and in cases that involved the trafficking of illegal immigrants from the Dominican Republic.

Gonzalo was interested in the connection between drugs and the immigrants, but he decided to let the DA follow the evidence and make the deals that might get someone to talk. When the missing half million dollars showed up, he turned it over to the DA, though he knew it might go missing within a week. He was tired and felt, justifiably, that he had done enough.

The money was found in the early morning when Collazo went to feed the Ortiz pigs. He got out of his truck at the front of the Ortiz property to speak with the Naranjito deputies watching the site and explain his presence.

"Another guy came in to feed them just about two minutes ago." one officer said.

"What was his name?"

"Carlos something. Not sure. Hector told us last night that someone was going to do it. He said it was all right to let him pass."

"Uh-huh. I'm the person. Let's go."

Carlos was in the shed looking for the burlap sacks Collazo had fed the pigs the day before. Collazo and the two officers came up from behind, surprising him.

"What do you want here, Carlos?" Collazo asked.

"There were sacks here . . ."

"I gave them to the pigs yesterday," Collazo said.

Carlos rushed past Collazo and the officers to the sty, where thick bundles of cash showed from the torn sacks. Some had been bitten, the rubber bands that had held them snapped. Fifty-dollar bills fluttered in the breeze.

"You know anything about this money?" Collazo asked.

Carlos hesitated, then said he only came to feed the pigs. He left in a hurry. He had an appointment to keep with the sheriff, he said.

Gonzalo made his flight to Paris in good time and did sleep on the plane as Mari had promised. He enjoyed his time with his daughters, visited castles he had never been to, and felt relaxed at the end of his allotted time away from responsibility.

Nobody called him with the news that after four days on life support and two operations, Jessica Ortiz died without ever having regained consciousness.